GW00854895

Copyright © 2021 Brianna Skylark

All rights reserved.

ISBN-13: 9781678952884

This is a work of fiction. Names, characters, places, and incidents either are the product of the author's imagination or are used fictitiously. Any resemblance to actual persons, living or dead, events, or locales is entirely coincidental.

Copyright © 2020 by Brianna Skylark.

All rights reserved. No part of this publication may be reproduced, distributed, or transmitted in any form or by any means, including photocopying, recording, or other electronic or mechanical methods, including information storage and retrieval systems, without the prior written permission of the author, except in the case of brief quotations embodied in critical reviews and certain other noncommercial uses permitted by copyright law.

First edition January 2020.

www.briannaskylark.com

COME WITH US

An Urban Foursome Vacation Romance

BRIANNA SKYLARK

*

Come With Us: An Urban Foursome Vacation Romance is the third book in the **Erotic Swingers** series and is the sequel to **Play With Us: An Urban Foursome Game Night Fantasy**. The first book in the series is **Be With Us: An Urban Foursome Love Story**. The fourth and final book is **Stay With Us: An Urban Foursome Swingers Ménage.**

Stories by Brianna Skylark

Erotic Swingers

Be With Us - An Urban Foursome Love Story

Play With Us - An Urban Foursome Game Night Fantasy

Come With Us - An Urban Foursome Vacation Romance

Stay With Us - An Urban Foursome Swingers Ménage

The Paramour - An Erotic Victorian Ménage

Taboo Fantasies

Tushie - A Taboo Tale of Forbidden Love

Muffin - A First Time FFM Ménage Romance

Bootie - A Hotwife Fantasy MFM Ménage

Cupcake - A Wife Swap Swingers Tale

Peach - A Penthouse Swingers Party

Petal - A Swingers Vacation Fantasy

The Billionaire's Naked Cleaner

Sweet and Discreet - Confessions of a Naked Cleaner

Sparkle and Spice - Adventures of a Naked Cleaner

Squeaky and Clean - Affairs of a Naked Cleaner

Naughty and Nice - The Billionaire's Naked Cleaner

First Time Swingers

Into the Swing - A First Time Wife Swap Fantasy

Back Swing - A Truth or Dare Swingers Fantasy

Hot Swing - A Hot Tub Swingers Fantasy

Mistletoe Swing - A Christmas Wife Swap Fantasy

Little Swing - An MFM Lockdown Ménage

Power Swing - A Billionaire Swingers Fantasy

First Time Fantasies

Fifth Base - A Cheeky First Time Fantasy

Sharing Rose - A Romantic MFM Mountain Ménage

Sun, sand, secrets and swinging.

Emilia, Cassian, Amy and Mark are jetting off to the Mediterranean to spend a few days in a secluded villa on a **cheeky summer vacation**, filled with sun, sand, secrets and **swinging**.

Amy's planned an entire week of *activities* for the **flirtatious foursome**, ticking off a **bucket list of naughty fantasies** along the way, including the opportunity for some threeway fun with Emilia after Cassian announces he can't get out of work and will have to join them a day late.

Emilia thinks the idea of a **secret night of passion** alone with Amy and Mark is too enticing to pass up, but when her stunning sister Alice appears that same evening on Cassian's doorstep back in Oxford, vulnerable and in need of a place to stay, the foursome are faced with the **biggest test of their relationship** yet...

Can they **survive temptation** and strengthen their love? Or will finally giving in to their *taboo* **desires** tear them apart forever?

*

CHAPTER ONE

Emilia gripped Amy's hand tight and closed her eyes, arching her head back as the intense vibrations throbbed through her hips. She reached out for Mark, fumbling for his hand as the crescendo grew, then stretched her toes and bit down on her lip, screwing her eyes closed tighter as the tempo increased.

Then it was happening.

Her stomach flipped and her whole body began to shake. There was a rushing sensation that seemed to overwhelm her senses, and then suddenly she felt lighter.

'You're doing fine, Em,' said Amy over the noise, 'Keep breathing. Do you want to open your eyes and take a look? It's beautiful.'

She shook her head as Mark stroked the back of her hand with his thumb.

'Amy's right,' he said, his voice deliberately calm and slow. 'There's no clouds up here.'

A bright beam of sunlight travelled quickly across her face, making her eyelids glow red. As it faded, she opened them apprehensively.

They were in the air.

'You did it,' said Amy, leaning into view from the window seat. 'See? That wasn't so bad.'

Emilia took a deep breath and focused her eyes beyond the silhouette of the beautiful redhead, looking out over the large wing of the aircraft and down thousands of feet onto the landscape of England below.

It was breathtaking.

A loud tone reverberated through the deck as the seatbelt sign turned off.

'What was that?' she said, looking around nervously, but Mark kept hold of her hand and nodded to his buckle before undoing it. She nodded satisfied, and settled back into the comfortable recliner.

'How are you feeling?' he said.

She puffed her lips and exhaled.

'Like I've just run a marathon.'

As she spoke, the plane tilted sharply, following its course as it turned south towards the coast and Emilia watched in amazement as she looked across the aisle and down at the ground out of the window.

From up here she could make out individual cars moving along on the M25 alongside houses tucked away down country lanes with pools and great landscaped gardens. It struck her that she had never truly appreciated just how beautiful England was before.

She remembered reading an article about how more than ninety-eight percent of the UK was green and just two percent had been built on. It seemed absurd at the time, but from up here she could believe it.

Her ears were starting to feel full and she yawned in an attempt to try and pop them, the left one pressurised easily, but the right one was stuck and was gradually becoming uncomfortable. She tilted her head and shook, pulling up the strap of her camisole top absentmindedly as she concentrated on relieving the sensation.

'What time does Cass's flight land tomorrow?' said Amy.

'Sorry?' she said, struggling to hear her as she kept forcibly yawning.

Amy reached down into the pocket of the seat in front and removed a lemon sherbet from a little paper bag she had tucked there before take off. As she bent forward, Emilia admired the little front buttoned summer dress she was wearing, and the slight glimpse of cleavage it afforded. It was easy to imagine her unbuttoning it later, and she stifled a smile at the thought.

'Have this,' she said, leaning back and producing the little yellow sweet. 'It'll help.'

Emilia took it gratefully and popped it into her mouth, taking Mark's hand again as she closed her eyes and sucked.

'When is Cass getting in tomorrow?' she said again.

'I think he lands at eleven in the morning.'

'Are we picking him up?'

Mark nodded from the other side. 'I was going to take the hire car to go get him, you girls can join me if you like?'

'He's really sorry he couldn't fly out with us,' said Emilia. 'He feels really bad.'

'We don't mind,' she laughed. 'We get to have you all to ourselves for a night,' she said, squeezing her hand delicately and then raising her eyebrows.

Emilia blushed and grinned as a nervous thrill tingled through her at the suggestion. She wasn't sure if Amy was serious though.

'Don't worry, we'll take care of you,' she said, seeing Emilia's face lined with worry.

'Sorry,' she looked down at her shaking knees. 'I'm not

good at flying.'

Emilia had only flown four times in her life. The first two times were on a family holiday to Majorca when she was six. All she could remember from the flight out was throwing up all over herself after drinking a cup of orange juice, sparking a life long aversion to the acidic drink. The last two times were on her honeymoon, and whilst the flight out had been reasonable, the return leg had been marred by turbulence. Six people had been injured after two overhead lockers fell open and the whole experience had scared her and made her even more anxious about being in the air.

The plane was filled with a mixture of retired couples, families with young children and business people. Towards the rear was a quite loud and excitable group of teenagers. Emilia wondered if they might be flying out to France on an exchange programme, preparing to spend their summer with another family down by the sea.

Even though she was struggling, her excitement about being away on holiday with Cassian, Mark and Amy overrode all of her anxieties. In fact she hadn't been this excited about travelling for years. They were now on route to Montpellier, where they would be hiring a car and driving along the mediterranean coast to a beautiful little village on the south side of Nîmes. She had always wanted to visit the Gard region, known across the world for its beautiful landscape, its Roman monuments and its rich history.

When Amy had invited them, she'd jumped at the opportunity, despite it meaning she would have to face her fear of flying head on.

But Cassian had been unable to get the day they were due to travel off work. An important deadline meant that he would be joining them the following morning on a separate flight. Emilia had originally suggested they both stay and head out to join Amy and Mark together, but Cassian had insisted that she go. The idea of travelling apart from her husband had set Emilia's anxiety off, but over the last two weeks she had worked herself up to the idea that it would be okay to travel with Amy and Mark.

It had also occurred to her how enjoyable it might be to spend a night alone with them. The idea hadn't been discussed though, not with Cassian, nor Amy or Mark, and now she was beginning to regret it.

She was so worried that her husband might say no, that she'd been too afraid to ask him. Now Amy seemed to be suggesting that they might be hoping she would join them this evening and her anxiety was back.

She wanted to talk to Cass all of a sudden, feeling silly that she hadn't done so already. Their communication as a couple had been incredible lately and she didn't want to let him down or hurt him. Their relationship had never been better.

She would call him later, and that would be okay.

If he said no, then she would respect that. It wasn't fair to presume otherwise.

She realised she had been chewing her lip and it was beginning to hurt. It was a habit that she'd had since childhood and she had developed a small callous behind her bottom lip as a result.

Amy glanced sideways at her and smiled, leaning across the arm to give her a quick kiss, making her smile and blush. In mild panic, she looked around to make sure no one else had seen. They squeezed each other's hand as the plane levelled out, another flash of sunlight brushing across their cheeks.

She took a deep breath, and smiled to herself as she remembered that whilst walking anxiously around the terminal building before boarding, she had seen and bought the sequel to *The Paramour*, the naughty book that her sister, Alice had loaned her a few months ago, the reading of which had led to her and Cassian meeting Amy and Mark at the masquerade ball in that gaudy and decadent mansion on the outskirts of Oxford. Reading it might help her relax.

It was in her overhead locker though, which meant standing up.

'Mark?' she said, nervously, indicating the row of baggage space above. 'Can I?'

'I can get it down? What are you after?'

'Erm, my book, and my phone?'

'Sure, no problem.'

She settled back into her seat and breathed. In a few minutes she would be lost again in the Scottish highlands, with Lady Victoria and the Duchess.

She could manage that.

Mark stood up and flipped open the locker, searching for her bag and finding it quickly and then lowering it down for her to rifle through. She grinned as she thought about the other men and women on the plane, looking up to see such a handsome man being a gentleman to her. He looked amazing, dressed in jeans and a simple button-up white shirt.

The book was easy to find but her phone was zipped inside an inner pocket next to her passport. After a moment or two of fumbling, she pulled it out and smiled.

'Thank you,' she said. As she moved her phone, the screen activated and she noticed she had four missed calls, all from her wild-child libertine sister, Alice.

She frowned, she hadn't heard her phone ring at all during boarding. Perhaps she'd called during take-off? She had a brief panic as she realised she'd not turned on airplane mode. Clearly the plane hadn't crashed however, so she calmed down and flicked it on.

Why had Alice called though, and *four* times?

'Everything okay?' said Amy, peering over.

'My sister rang, I don't know why though.'

'Is that unusual?'

'She doesn't normally *keep* calling,' Emilia showed Amy the missed calls.

'I'm sure she's fine, maybe she's forgotten you're flying out today?'

'Maybe.'

But she was worried. Whilst she'd been looking at her phone, she'd left her book out on the little tray table and Amy was peering curiously at the cover.

'What are you reading?'

She grinned and blushed, placing her hand over it. 'You can't laugh.'

'Well now I'm *really* intrigued.'

Mark turned his head to look down at the cover, his interest piqued, but Emilia flipped it over and concealed it, spreading her fingers wide.

'Don't start hiding things from us, Em,' laughed Amy. 'There shouldn't be any secrets between us.'

She shook her head and grinned. 'All right fine,' she said. 'But it's better than one might assume.'

'One assume's nothing, my dear.'

'Stop it!'

'What *is* it?'

Emilia turned it back over, slowly.

'*The Paramour's Lover*,' said Amy, curiously, then she gasped. 'I've heard of this.'

She picked up the book from Emilia's little table and turned it over to read the blurb.

'Isn't there another one?'

'This is the sequel. I didn't know it was out.'

She flicked through the pages and stopped on a random one, gasping and grinning as she read out loud.

'Victoria *began to unlace the strings of her corset as* Elizabeth *looked on, her heaving bos-*'.

Emilia snatched the paperback back out her hands. 'Stop!' she said, shaking her head as she laughed. 'You're so mean.'

'I'm sorry,' said Amy, wrinkling her nose as Mark shook his head at her.

'You should read it,' she said, defiant. 'It's actually very *good*. There is a story too.'

'Ok,' she said, nodding. 'I will. If you like it, then I'm sure I'll like it. We share an interest in husbands, we'll probably like the same books.'

Emilia laughed. 'I'd like that. I can lend you the first one? It's a bit… used.'

'Should I give it a wipe down first?' laughed Amy.

Mark's eyes widened and he looked away, pretending he wasn't listening, but Amy saw.

'Don't despair now dear husband, you've got a whole week of this to come,' she said, leaning forward.

'Do you mind if I read for a little while?' said Emilia.

'Of course not,' said Amy. 'And don't worry about Alice, I'm sure she's fine. You can call her when we land.'

Emilia smiled. 'Thank you,' then she whispered. 'I love you.'

'I love you too,' Amy paused for a moment, looking out the window before turning back. 'I'm so glad we met.'

Emilia looked up at her and smiled.

'Us too.'

Amy picked up her magazine and opened it up to a celebrity gossip article as Mark put his head back and closed his eyes.

Emilia looked down at the cover of her book and thought about her sister again.

Alice was always the one she went to for advice, but it was rarely reciprocated. She was the older one, wiser, more capable, more experienced… In many ways. To have called her four times in short succession was out of character.

She sighed and opened her book. For now, she needed to escape… From the plane, from missing Cassian, and from worrying about her sister.

She flipped open the first page, and began to read.

*

The hire car that Mark had booked was not designed for luggage.

It was sporty, sleek and almost entirely form over function. Amy and Emilia stood in the multi-storey, their suitcases by their sides, staring at it.

'It was a great deal,' he laughed as he opened the boot and threw his bag in. 'It was the only one they had at short notice with enough seats for four adults, I'm afraid.'

'Yeah, right,' said Amy, laughing.

'Gosh if we ever have kids we'll need a minibus,' said Emilia.

Mark half laughed, but Amy remained silent, a hesitant smile on her face as Emilia stopped breathing, realising what she'd just said.

'Sorry, I was just making a joke.'

The three of them stood awkwardly and Mark began to close the boot before realising the girls luggage was still on the concrete.

'It's okay, I just hadn't really thought about that before,' said Amy, breaking the silence.

'Me neither,' lied Emilia. 'I just-'.

'It's fine,' she said, shaking her head.

'Let me take that,' said Mark, hefting Emilia's oversized suitcase into the boot. The suspension complained, groaning audibly as he hefted it in.

'Front or back?' said Amy, smiling at her friend.

'You're both welcome to travel in the back if you like? I

don't mind playing chauffeur,' he shrugged. 'I do it every day.'

'Shall we?' said Amy.

Emilia nodded, thankful for the change in topic.

Mark held the door open for them both, Amy clambering over to the far seat as Emilia stepped in behind her.

The car was sleek inside and seemed to have been sculpted into curves and hollows, there was even two touchscreen tablets embedded into the back of the front seats. It was so comfortable that Emilia felt like she was sinking into the moulded recliners. As Mark started the engine, Amy reached across and took hold of her hand, squeezing it tight.

'*We're on holiday together,*' she said, her eyes wide with excitement and happiness. 'Oh, you could call Alice now?'

'Oh, yes. Do you think my phone will work?'

'Should do,' said Mark. 'Same tariff as you get at home.'

'Is it okay if I call her?'

'Please do, it's important.'

Emilia pulled her phone out of her carry on bag and tapped to call as they left the underground car park, the bright sunshine making her squint as they rolled out of the lower level.

After a long moment of silence, a strange single tone rang through her ears. She was busy.

'Don't put it down, it's not engaged,' said Mark, looking at her through the rear view mirror. 'The dial tone is different here.'

Emilia nodded, and it kept going. After a while it went to voice mail and Emilia cancelled the call.

'She's not answering.'

'I'm sure she's fine,' said Amy, trying to sound reassuring.

'I could make a call to one of my guys?' said Mark. 'Get someone to go and check on her if you like?'

Emilia blinked. 'You can do that?'

He nodded, glancing at her in the rear view mirror.

'No, not yet,' she said after considering the idea. 'I don't want to freak her out.'

They turned off a small roundabout and began heading down a slip road with Mark accelerating onto the motorway and joining a line of fast moving cars with ease, confidence and precision. He drove like he moved, fast but with a fastidious intensity. Emilia found it exhilarating, and just a little scary.

She squeezed Amy's hand tighter as the sleek vehicle shot forward, the speed pressing her back into her seat and making her feel giddy.

'What about Cass?' said Amy, seemingly unfazed. 'Would he able to find out what's wrong?'

'Maybe,' Emilia unlocked her phone again and tapped on Cassian's number, listening to the strange dial tone once more, but it just rang and rang and rang.

She was beginning to worry now. Cassian rarely, if ever, failed to answer his phone. He did so much of his work through it that it barely ever left his face, let alone his side.

It kept on ringing.

Something was wrong, but she wasn't sure what.

Should she call her mum and dad? Were they okay? Had something happened to one of them? But if she did call and everything was fine, she'd worry them too.

The dial tone stopped and Emilia held her breath, waiting for Cassian's voice.

'Did he answer?' said Amy, quietly.

She shook her head as his answerphone message began to play.

*

As they'd neared the villa, the roads had gradually become

more rural and Mark had been forced to slow down as they'd crept along narrow streets running through beautiful historical towns and tight tree lined roads that snaked between old villages.

Occasional boarded up houses, isolated in the middle of nowhere crawled by as Emilia looked out at them wondering who might once have lived there and why they'd left it abandoned as nature had reclaimed it, breaking the stone walls with the roots of trees and plants as the ceilings collapsed inward from years of seasonal erosion.

She'd watched a documentary last year about all of the abandoned holiday homes across Europe, particularly in Spain. Homes purchased as retirement properties for elderly ex-pats, leaving the houses to their children who would then cease to maintain or visit them. Some of them were simply lost, with inheritors not having records of addresses or deeds. Perhaps some of these properties had suffered the same fate? Lost to apathy.

Their holiday villa was bordered by an eight foot tall wall and a proximity gate with a sensor linked to the keys that Mark had collected from the travel agent in Oxford. The driveway alone was longer than Emilia and Cassian's entire street and it was lined with trees which created a canopy of shadow over the gravel track. Above the walls Emilia could see palm trees and bamboo plants swaying in the gentle breeze.

It looked like a private paradise.

She looked again at her phone, her excitement tempered by worry.

Neither her sister, nor Cassian had got back to her still.

As they approached the gate it opened slowly and Mark rolled the powerful car through, the soft sound of the gravel beneath the tires felt soothing somehow as he slowed to a halt in front of the main entrance.

'Oh my goodness,' said Amy.

Mark flashed a smile and turned off the engine, gesturing both arms out theatrically.

'Bienvenue, to your home away from home.'

'You speak French?' said Emilia, leaning forward.

'Of course he does,' said Amy, as she clicked open the side door. 'And German, Spanish, Cantonese and Japanese. Over-achieving little shit.'

'I speak French and Spanish fluently,' he said, correcting his wife as he unclipped his seatbelt. 'The others are passable. I'm still learning.'

'That's amazing,' said Emilia as Amy pushed open her door and stepped out onto the driveway. She could feel the heat of the sun immediately, like the inside of an oven.

'It's gorgeous out here,' she said, beckoning to them both. 'Come on.'

Mark stepped out and Emilia followed, feeling the full force of the sun's heat the moment she alighted.

'Gosh,' she said.

'Bit warm?' laughed Amy.

Mark walked to the rear of the car and popped open the boot, smiling as it rose softly and eased to a halt. He picked up the girl's bags first, leaving his own, and then headed towards the front door.

'I'm hoping the air conditioning is on a timer,' he said as he pushed the key into the lock and turned it. There was a soft click and the door unlocked, gently opening as he picked up the bags again, then smiling as cool air drifted out and over him.

'Thank goodness for that.'

It was dark inside as the external shutters were all closed to keep the heat out, and as Mark had hoped, the air conditioning was on a timer keeping the place at an even temperature even in the height of summer.

Emilia stepped across the threshold, holding Amy's hand and peering a little nervously into the darkness. The acoustics were hollow from the tiled floors and the stone walls and her eyes were still adjusting from the bright sunlight outside so she felt quite disoriented as she followed the couple in.

'Which room would you and Cassian like?' called Mark from up ahead in the darkness.

Amy found a light switch. She tapped it and low level floor lights faded up, lining the corridor and revealing Mark rather theatrically.

'I don't mind,' she called back, smiling as she looked around.

Amy approached her and slipped her arms around her waist, standing on tip toes to kiss her.

'We're here,' she said. 'I'm so pleased you came.'

'Me too,' said Emilia, grinning back and then looking down at the floor, worry creasing her brow.

'They'll be fine,' said Amy, placing one palm on her cheek. 'Maybe it's just something simple like a phone tower has gone down.'

'I hadn't thought of that,' she said, looking up and smiling weakly. 'I hope it's something like that.'

'Let's leave our bags here and go take a look around shall we?' she reached out and took ahold of Emilia's free hand.

'Ok,' she said, nodding. She stood her luggage upright and laughed as Amy tugged her along excitedly and through a curved archway into another darkened but larger space.

The lights came on as they entered, fading up gently and revealing a beautiful lounge and dining area. In the centre there were two couches facing each other, long enough to seat four people on each. Perpendicular at either end were two more arm chairs. In the centre was a huge glass coffee table, above which was a stunning crystal chandelier attached to a thick wooden beamed ceiling.

The rear wall was made of sliding patio doors, with external wooden shutters lining the other side. Amy let go of her hand and rushed over to open them, unlocking and then sliding the partition back. Emilia began to do the same on the other side, and together they opened the first shutter letting the sunlight flood in.

The overhead lights turned off automatically but the girls barely noticed as they stared out with wide eyes into the courtyard of the villa. Before them lay a large wooden deck complete with an outdoor covered dining area and a number of deck chairs and loungers.

Amy stepped out onto the decking, taking hold of Emilia's hand again.

'Oh my goodness,' she said. 'Look at that.'

Beyond the decking was a small tropical garden area, with palm trees, beautiful bright flowers, white stepping stones and a border of potted plants and carefully shaped bushes that had been carved into little dome shapes. But next to that, was the pool.

Amy laughed as she took it all in. The still water on the surface glistened and sparkled, inviting them to leap in and they both had to hold themselves back from doing so.

The end nearest to them was curved with small steps leading down into a shallow area which quickly appeared to deepen in the middle. At the far end was a stepped area which led up to a submerged platform with curved sides where you could sit together, just beneath the water and stay cool in the heat of the day.

'This is incredible,' said Emilia looking around, glancing up at the palm trees swaying in the light breeze.

Mark appeared behind them and slipped his arm around Amy.

'What do you think?' he said.

'It's beautiful,' she turned around and wrapped her arms

around him, then glanced across at Emilia as she pressed her cheek into his chest and swayed.

'I'm going to get unpacked and then shall we have something to eat?' he said, to both of them.

'Yes, definitely,' said Amy. 'I'm starving. Plane food is stingy.'

Emilia nodded happily and smiled as Mark peeled away, turning back and stepping in through the glass partition and back into the shadows of the villa.

The two girls looked at each other, with Amy grinning wildly and then looking down with a sudden shyness, hesitantly licking her lips as she walked over slowly and nervously.

'Listen,' said Amy, sliding her arms up and around Emilia's neck. As she spoke, she started to blush. 'I was hoping, that maybe, if you want to, you could come and stay with us tonight... in our bed?'

Emilia felt butterflies flood into her tummy again and her neck started to radiate heat as she blushed too. 'I'd really like that,' she said quietly, smiling. 'But I should ask Cass first.'

Amy nodded enthusiastically. 'Of course you should, it's only fair. Mark is very excited, *and*, he said he would be happy to return the favour and leave us alone for a night with Cassian if you'd like that?'

'I'd really like that too,' she grinned and breathed in deeply. The two of them kissed again, holding each other tight.

'I love you, you know?' said Emilia into Amy's ear.

'You've mentioned it once or twice.'

'Thank you for this.'

'Thank you for coming. Now go unpack and take your mind of Cass and Alice,' she said, stepping back as Emilia smiled softly.

'Ok, I will,' she said as she crossed the threshold of the

glass doors, following the noise of Mark unpacking and opening shutters further inside.

'Emilia?' said Amy, calling after her.

She stopped and looked back at the redhead, silhouetted in the bright sunlight of the open door.

'I love you too.'

*

The evening air was still warm as Emilia stood in the little tropical garden and stretched her legs. Even the grass beneath her feet seemed baked, trapped by the intense heat of the Mediterranean sun.

It was already getting late. Instead of unpacking she'd decided to lay down on the large king size bed in the room she had chosen for herself and Cassian and she had quickly fallen asleep, dozing in the warmth of the afternoon.

By the time she'd woken up the sun was setting and she'd wandered out to the garden to watch the golden hues fade to orange and then blue.

The world around her was alive and teeming with life, and yet they were so isolated here that she could already see more stars above her than she had ever seen before.

She'd never appreciated just how much light pollution there was above the skies of Oxford, and the absence was dizzying. As her eyes adjusted she could just make out the faint edges of the milky way. Here the stars seemed to flash, some with a hint of red, others blue and some seemed to move gently in the sky as though they were drifting in an infinite ocean.

The surrounding fields were filled with the sound of crickets, a cacophony of noise that seemed to rise and fall like a murmur of birds. She'd never heard anything like it before. She was so used to the background noise of traffic and trains that she had no idea nature could be so loud.

The only light aside from the stars came from the small solar powered lanterns which lined the edge of the pool, casting a golden sparkling shimmer on the waters gently rippling surface.

It was humbling.

She stifled a grin, and tried to quell a sudden surge of arousal, placing her fingers on her lips as she looked down at the floor and crossed her legs, squeezing herself tight.

Amy was in the shower.

She could hear the sound of the pump, vibrating through the walls. She could hear Mark too, preparing them something which smelled amazing for dinner.

She missed Cassian.

She felt her phone vibrate in her back pocket and reached for it, hoping to see his name, but it was blank, her eyes struggling to adjust to the brightness of the screen.

A phantom ring. She'd been getting them more and more recently. She wondered if it was a sign of addiction or a muscle issue, either way it was a nuisance and a source of frequent disappointment.

She still hadn't heard from him or Alice. Nothing since they'd taken off, and she was more than a little worried now

What if he'd had an accident? What if he was hurt? And why hadn't Alice called back?

She should call him again.

Besides, she wanted to ask him about tonight. It was only fair if she asked. But she was worried that she might not like the answer.

But what if he didn't pickup? She chewed her lip and took a deep breath, then hit dial.

After a few seconds, the call connected. For a moment she thought the line was busy again as the dialling tone was so different to the one she was used to, but then she remembered and settled and waited.

Something flapped through the air above her, and she instinctively ducked, listening as it disappeared into the night.

Bats.

She didn't want to go inside, she wanted to talk to Cass privately, but the idea of standing out in the open as bats flapped around just feet above her head was too much. She looked around and then walked quickly towards a little metal table with a parasol near the far end the pool.

The phone stopped ringing.

'Hi, you've reached the mailbox of Cassian Black, please leave your name and number and I'll get back to you as soon as I can.'

'Shit,' she said aloud. 'Where is he?'

She pressed the screen and then opened up the Find Your Family app. Cass had installed it for her so she could track his journey home to stop her worrying about whether he was okay.

She tapped on his name and waited, watching the little circle whirl.

Nothing.

Then her phone rang.

With relief she read his name and answered.

'Hey,' she said.

'Hey beautiful,' said Cassian, a slight delay on the line. 'Made it there safe?'

'I was well looked after,' she smiled, nodding, thankful to hear his voice at last. 'I've been really worried about you.'

'Are you at the villa?'

'Yes, it's beautiful,' she looked around. 'The pool is gorgeous, it's all lit up with solar lamps, and oh my goodness it's so hot here, but there is air-con. Are you okay? What's been going on?'

'Yeah, I'm good, listen, your sister's here,' said Cassian.

Emilia's stomach tightened and she sat up straight.

'What? Why? Is she okay?'

'Yeah, she's okay, she didn't realise you were away. She's pretty upset, something happened at work, but I'll let her explain.'

'Can I talk to her?'

'She's upstairs at the moment,' said Cassian, then there was a long pause. 'She's getting a shower.'

'She's a getting a shower?'

'Yeah,' he said.

'And you're downstairs?'

'Yes,' he said, firmly.

There was another long pause, and then Emilia started to laugh. She bent forward on her chair as she continued to giggle down the phone.

'Oh my goodness, your wife is in another country and her incredibly hot, promiscuous sister, who has a *massive* crush on you, is upstairs, wet, naked and vulnerable right now. How are you even coping?'

There was a final, lengthy pause before she heard Cassian exhale unsteadily.

'Not great,' he said, his voice wavering.

'Oh gosh, you should go upstairs, walk in and be like,' she put on a deep voice. '*Need a hand?*'

'I don't think that would go down as well as you're imagining,' said Cassian, laughing quietly. 'Besides I think she's out now, the showers off.'

'Missed your window of opportunity there.'

Emilia heard Alice say something in the background.

'She's coming down now.'

'Dressed in a towel?'

'Yep.'

'The smallest one we have?'

'Yep.'

'I can't the imagine the look on your face right now. You should probably sit down.'

'Yep.'

There was some quiet muttering, then Alice's voice came down the line.

'Hey, Em,' she said, loudly. 'I'm sorry. I forgot you guys were heading off on your swingers tour of the Med.'

'It's not a tour,' she said, laughing.

'So did you forget Cass?' she laughed. 'He's not a dog you know?'

'He's joining us tomorrow.'

'Nice, some alone time with Prince Charming and Cinderella for you tonight then?'

'It's not like that,' said Emilia, but she could feel herself going red and hoping Cassian was out of earshot.

'Of course it is, I can practically hear you blushing.'

'Stop it,' she laughed quietly. 'So what's wrong? You don't normally pop round for a shoulder to cry on.'

'I got fired,' she said.

'Oh.'

'And evicted.'

'*Oh.*'

'Yeah.'

'What happened?'

'It doesn't matter,' she said. 'The long and short of it is don't piss off an oligarch.'

Emilia frowned. 'How did you piss off a Russian billionaire?'

'It's best you don't know.'

'Are you safe?'

'Yes, I'm with Cass.'

'What are you going to do?'

'Win,' said Alice, laughing. 'I don't know how to lose.'

'Please be careful.'

Emilia listened closely as the line went quiet. She could hear Alice breathing, then she spoke.

'Do you remember how we used to play chess when we were little?'

'Yes I know,' said Emilia, exasperated. 'You don't think like other people. But this is not the same, Alice.'

'I can handle it.'

Emilia huffed. 'I know, I just worry about you.'

'I can handle it.'

'Listen, stay the night with Cass. Don't go disturbing mum and dad, it's late and they'll get worried. You can stay at ours until you sort something out.'

'Is that okay?'

'Of course,' she said, smiling again. 'We're away until Saturday, so you've got the place to yourself. If you need cash, there's some in the safe upstairs. You can guess the code. There's plenty of frozen food in the freezer so just help yourself.'

'Thank you,' she said.

'Cass will look after you, if you need anything tonight.'

There came a short laugh from the other side. 'Anything?' said Alice, suggestively.

Emilia grinned, but as she was about to make a snarky retort, she paused and frowned, then she shook her head and took a deep breath.

'Yes. *Anything*.' There was silence from the other end. 'Just don't wear him out. I want him firing on all cylinders tomorrow night.'

There was another long pause, followed by quiet giggling. The next word came as a whisper.

'Really?'

Emilia's stomach tightened, and her chest constricted. Her whole body seemed to flush with heat and goosebumps broke out along the skin of her arms and neck. She took a deep breath and a thousand thoughts ran through her mind in a matter of seconds.

The idea was utterly and completely wrong, and yet she'd joked about it for years. She knew they both wanted each other. She knew they had harboured feelings for one another for over a decade. Cassian had joked about it. Alice had joked about it. And on more than one occasion, Emilia had voiced her approval of it.

But now the joke seemed *real*.

She was nearly a thousand miles away, under a different sky, hoping that tonight she would make love with Mark and Amy in the humid warmth of their room, and wake up tomorrow morning naked between her girlfriend's thighs as Mark made them a continental breakfast of croissants and coffee.

The trouble was she hadn't talked to Cassian about it.

She should've done, but somehow, it had seemed like a huge deal.

'Look, I'm not telling you to get off the phone, drop your towel and bend over the dining room table. I'm just saying, I love you both. If the situation arises, you don't have to say no. I want you to be happy.'

Emilia's heart fluttered as she said the words out loud. It didn't seem real. As though they were being said by someone else.

'How do you know I'm in a towel?' said Alice, quietly down the phone.

'Cass mentioned it.'

'Did he now? Interesting.'

'*Alice.*'

'I love you,' she giggled.

'I love you too, now put my husband back on, you dirty cheating whore.'

Her sister burst into laughter as she called for Cassian.

'Hi Em,' she heard him say, as he cleared his throat.

'Can you go somewhere private?' she said, straight away.

'Erm, sure. Hang on.'

She listened, shaking with a mixture of excitement and arousal as Cassian made his way to what sounded like the back garden decking.

'Ok, I'm outside.'

'Alice needs somewhere to stay for tonight and a maybe a little while longer.'

'Ok,' he said, she could almost hear him frowning with curiosity.

'That's not what I wanted to talk to you about though.'

'Oh.'

'I miss you.'

'I miss you too.'

'You're so good to me. You're always looking after me,' she smiled but then she hesitated. 'I don't know how to say this.'

'You want to know if I mind you having fun with Amy and Mark, without me there.'

Emilia stayed silent for as long as Cassian paused, waiting for his response.

'No, I don't mind,' he said at last.

Her whole body sagged as all the tension she had allowed to build was released. She breathed deeper and more completely than she had done in what felt like hours, then she laughed.

'I love you,' she said.

'I love you too.'

'Do you think there's something wrong with us?'

Cassian laughed. 'What do you mean?'

'I'm in the south of France, hoping I'm about to have a threesome with a married couple and you're back home, probably about to fuck my sister in our bed.'

'What?'

'You heard me.'

'I'm not going to fuck Alice.'

'You can though, if you want to? She wants you to.'

'What? She said that?'

'Sort of.'

'What did you say?'

'What do you think I said?'

'I don't know, I'm not psychic.'

'I said *yes*.'

There followed a silence. It went on for so long, Emilia wondered if they'd been cut off, but then she heard him breathing. 'Really?'

There was that feeling again. The heat in her chest. The goosebumps on her arms.

This was it, her last chance to change her mind.

'Yes,' she said. '*Really*.'

*

CHAPTER TWO

Emilia tucked her phone into the back pocket of her jeans and stepped carefully over the threshold of the sliding rear doors of the villa.

It was cooler inside the building. The air conditioning had been on for a while now and the temperature had dropped enough that it almost felt cold. Mark seemed to like it that way and she smiled as she thought about how different he and Amy were sometimes.

The lights were off in the living room, so she meandered her way slowly towards the hallway that led to the kitchen, listening to Amy chatting cheerfully with her husband.

As she passed the leather sofa she brushed her fingers along the top. It felt warm to the touch. She wondered if it was real or faux, scratching her nails softly into the textured finish.

Her mind was preoccupied with the conversation she'd just had. She was struggling to understand her own emotions. A few weeks ago, life was simple, but something was missing.

Now she felt complete.

But a part of her kept telling herself that all of this was wrong. Not by her standards, but by everyone else's. That if her mother were to find out, she wouldn't approve.

She couldn't take Amy and Mark home to meet her parents. *Hi mum, this is Amy, she's my girlfriend. This is her husband, he's my boyfriend. Oh and you already know, Cassian. Surprise, we're polyamorous now! P.S. Cassian and Alice are fucking too.*

That last part was the bit she was struggling to reconcile.

She *should* feel sick with jealously, that right now, her husband and her sister might be about to make love in their marital bed. Instead she felt compassion and love.

She wanted them to be together, they wanted each other after all and who was she to say they couldn't be physical together? Who was she to say who her husband had coffee with? Or played squash with? And for that matter, who he fucked? He wasn't her property, and neither was she. And why wouldn't she be happy that two people she loved, would want to share their love with one another?

The idea was thrilling.

That right now they could be wrapped in each other's arms, making love?

She couldn't help feeling as if something was *wrong* with her though. As though if she told someone they would become angry and demand to know what her problem was.

Should she tell Amy and Mark? She didn't want them to be angry at her. But like Amy had said on the plane, *There shouldn't be any secrets between us.* It was a joke at the time, but it was true. There shouldn't be any secrets. The foundation of their new relationship was based on trust. Honesty, openness and trust. She'd never been happier, but everything somehow felt more precarious now.

Amy had described something similar to her a few weeks back. How during their game night, as Cassian was fucking her from behind in the dark corridor of their home, she could hear Mark and herself in the lounge, making love, and instead of feeling anger or resentment, she had been filled with joy and compassion.

It was as though by opening up their relationship, not only had all their preconceptions of love and monogamy been challenged, they had been smashed to pieces. But the key to all of it, the single link in the chain that held it all together, was communication and honesty. If the trust was broken, it all fell apart.

Amy's laugh interrupted her thoughts and she smiled, enjoying the sound of her girlfriend's voice as it drifted through the villa.

It was strange, being in love with more than one person, but it felt *right*. That was another preconception that had been shattered. The idea that her heart could love just one person, that somehow she would fill it with love until it was full and that was that. It turned out that the more she loved, the more her heart seemed to *grow*. Now it felt like it was bursting.

She took a deep breath. Cassian was as much a part of their new relationship as she was. Yes, she was here, and he was at home, but that didn't make her more important. She had to tell them, honestly and openly what she had agreed to. What she had *suggested*. They should be a part of that decision and if they were uncomfortable with it, then she would call Cassian back.

She walked out of the lounge and along the corridor, breathing slowly and preparing herself, stopping a few feet away from the open door and closing her eyes, before stepping through into the light of the kitchen.

'Hey sweetie,' said Amy. 'Did you get through?'

Emilia laughed. 'I did, I think he's doing pretty well.'

'Is he missing you?'

'Not tonight,' she smiled knowingly. 'My sisters with him.'

Amy raised her eyebrows and laughed. 'Oh gosh. Is she okay?'

'I don't know,' said Emilia. 'She got fired today. She also said something about pissing off an oligarch?'

Mark frowned and turned to her as she spoke, curious.

'What is it she does again?'

'She's a corporate accountant.'

'How does a corporate accountant piss off an oligarch?'

'I have no idea, I don't really understand what she does. She travels all over the world, doing financial consultancy work for various firms. Her most recent account was in Moscow.'

'Where did she study?'

'Oxford.'

Mark raised his eyebrows and grinned, turning back to the cooking.

'What?' she said.

'Nothing,' he laughed.

Emilia frowned and carried on. 'She's going to stay at ours for a while, whilst she sorts herself out.'

'That's good,' said Amy. 'Do you think we'll get to meet her when we get back?'

'Yeah, I'd like that,' she said. 'She's hardly ever around, so now's a good time. Although she'll have probably moved on by the time we're all home.'

'How will you introduce us?' grinned Amy, raising her eyebrows.

'She already knows.'

Amy's expression dropped. 'Oh, really?'

Emilia laughed. 'Yeah.'

Mark turned his head, nodding and smiling. 'Bold move.'

'How did you tell her?'

Emilia went red and took a deep breath. 'Well, actually she was at the masquerade party that night.'

'She was?'

'She gave us the tickets,' shrugged Emilia.

'Is she married?' asked Mark.

'No, in fact she's always had a bit of a thing for Cass.'

'I don't blame her,' laughed Amy.

'That's kind of what I wanted to talk to you about.'

Amy frowned, and Mark turned his head back as he stirred.

'About your sister's crush on Cass?'

She nodded and took a deep breath. 'Ok, this is going to sound weird.'

Amy laughed nervously as Emilia continued.

'So Cass and Alice have always had a thing for each other. We all went to school together and she was in the same year as him, so we've all known each other since forever but I've always known that she likes him. She's not subtle about it, she quite openly tells me she fantasises about him and is always joking about fucking him behind my back, but she never would. Not without my *permission*.'

Amy stared at her, waiting for her to finish and then realised that she had.

'I don't understand,' she said, turning to Mark as he looked back at the pan and then back to Emilia who smiled awkwardly.

'I've always said that they could sleep together if they wanted, and that they should just fuck one day and get it out of their system and that I wouldn't mind.'

'Ok?'

'She's at home with him tonight.'

Amy's jaw dropped.' You think they're going to have *sex* tonight?'

'I said they could, if they wanted.'

Mark stopped stirring and turned around as Amy's eyes went wide. 'You're okay with that?'

Emilia nodded slowly. 'Are you both okay with it?'

'I don't think it has anything to do with us,' said Amy, confused. 'She's your sister?'

'I know, but we're all in this now. If you don't feel comfortable with it, then you can say and I'll call him back.'

'Do *you* feel comfortable with it?'

'I think so.'

'You think so?'

'Yes.'

Amy took a deep breath and huffed, rubbing her eyes. 'I take it back, you are an *eleven* on the crazy-hot scale.'

Mark laughed and carried on stirring.

'So does that mean you're okay with it?'

'If *you* are sweetie, then yes I am, I'm not sure I understand though.'

Emilia looked down at her feet and then back up at Amy, trying to find the right words.

'It's like you said at our house on the game night, I should be clawing her eyes out, but instead I'm just really happy for them.'

Amy nodded and after staring for a few moments, she opened her arms, inviting Emilia for a hug.

She took a few unsteady steps towards her and they embraced.

'You are crazy, but I love you,' whispered Amy.

Emilia pulled back and smiled. 'So, what's for dinner?'

'Ratatouille,' said Mark, continuing to stir. He dipped the wooden spoon into the pot and came out with a small amount, turning and holding it up to Emilia's lips for her to taste.

She delicately accepted, doing her best not to spill any.

'Oh my goodness, that's good,' she nodded, dabbing at the hot sauce around her mouth.

Amy leaned up and kissed her, running her tongue along her lips as she tasted the flavour.

'Wouldn't want to waste any,' she giggled, laughing as she turned away.

'Shall we?' said Mark. 'It's ready.'

Amy nodded, grabbing three plates and some cutlery.

'Can you grab the wine glasses, Em?'

Emilia followed Mark through to the dining area as Amy fluttered past, laying the table and singing softly as she did so.

'You sing beautifully,' said Emilia, smiling as she listened and stepping aside as Mark returned to the kitchen.

'Don't be daft, but you're very kind to say. Mark, can you bring the salt and pepper?'

'It doesn't need any,' he shouted. 'And yes, she has a beautiful voice.'

'You do,' laughed Emilia.

'Can you bring the salt and pepper anyway?' shouted Amy, ignoring them both.

Mark appeared at the doorway a second later, holding salt, pepper and a carafe of wine, wiggling them all and smiling with a wry grin. He placed the grinders down in front of his wife and then poured out three glasses of red. The girls took their seats and as Mark sat down, he raised his up.

'To unconventional relationships,' he said.

Amy clinked hers and Emilia followed suit, then tucked into her dish, plunging her fork into the assorted vegetables and taking a delicate bite, blushing as the flavour permeated her taste buds. Discovering that Mark was an incredible cook somehow made him even more attractive and she was already struggling to keep her hands off him, not that Amy would mind, but she felt like a guest right now and she didn't want to push their boundaries.

There was a part of her that wanted to slide her dish aside, crawl across the table and kiss them both one after the other. Instead she crossed her legs and squeezed, trying to stem her gradually increasing arousal.

What was going to happen after they finished eating?

Would Mark take them both by the hand through to the bedroom? Would Amy kiss her first? Would they have pudding or a drink beforehand?

She didn't want to make the first move. She hadn't even told them that Cassian had said yes yet.

She felt like she was back in school again, staring up at teenage floppy haired Cassian as he talked to her, as though he wasn't the only thing in her world at that moment in time, paralysed by his presence and unable to bring herself to tell him how she felt.

She stopped her train of thought.

They were both looking at her.

'Did you hear what I said?' asked Amy, smiling as she wiped her lips.

'No, I'm sorry,' she looked at her and then Mark, embarrassed.

'Lost in thought?'

Emilia nodded. 'What did you say?'

'What would you like to do tomorrow? After Cass get's here?'

'Oh, erm. I don't know. Are there choices?'

Mark nodded, swallowing. 'We could grab some dinner in the village? Or have a night in or a paddle in the pool?'

'Night in sounds nice,' she said, trying to hide her expression behind another forkful of vegetables. '*And* a paddle in the pool?'

'I'd like that too,' said Amy.

'Oh, could we go into the city one day and visit the

Colosseum?' said Emilia, suddenly.

'Yeah, we could fit that in,' said Mark, nodding.

'Could we? I've always wanted to go there. It's the most well preserved Roman Amphitheatre in the world.'

Mark nodded. 'Built almost two thousand years ago, around twenty years after the Colosseum of Rome.'

Emilia smiled. 'Are you into ancient history?'

'No,' said Amy laughing. 'He went to a Metallica concert there.'

'I *worked* a Metallica concert there thank you, and yes, I'm interested in ancient history, particularly Roman. This whole area is rich in historical Roman culture, the city was once a regional capital.'

Amy took another swig of wine and grinned at Emilia who immediately felt under the spotlight and frowned.

'So, Em,' said Amy tilting her head. 'Was I the second person you ever kissed?'

Emilia immediately blushed and took a mouthful of ratatouille, looking down in embarrassment.

'Amy,' said Mark, admonishing her.

'Oh my goodness,' she said, holding a hand up to her mouth. 'I was, wasn't I?'

Emilia squirmed and hid her face, looking out into the garden as she went bright red. She took a deep breath and then nodded.

Amy jumped up and rounded the table, coming into her line of sight, but Emilia looked away again.

'Em, I'm so sorry, I'm really flattered,' she said, trying to get her to uncover her face, instead she just wrapped her arms around her on the stool and hugged her tight.

Mark took a deep breath and laughed, taking another mouthful down as he looked at them both.

Emilia relented and embraced Amy, reaching out and holding her around her waist as she danced back and forth.

'That's amazing,' she said, finally making eye contact with her again, before glancing at Mark. 'You are so cute.'

Mark nodded grinning as Amy's expression changed from excited to pensive, she looked down at Emilia again and took a deep breath, holding her hands a little tighter as she spoke.

'So, erm. Did you ask Cassian about, you know, tonight?'

Emilia smiled and blushed, then nodded.

'What did he say?'

She looked at them both in turn, her face bright red and then nodded again.

Amy's eyes seemed to sparkle. Emilia thought for a moment that she might jump up and down on the spot but instead she stayed still, just swaying in her hands and smiling.

She glanced back across the table at Mark who was finishing his last mouthful. Amy's plate was already clear. She had noticed that she had wolfed it down whereas her husband had been taking his time, keeping pace with her, not wanting to rush.

Now he stood up, slowly and confidently. It was measured, and practiced. She could easily imagine that if he made the same motion in a room full of powerful executives or politicians, they would've all been silenced.

Amy and Emilia looked at him as he stood stolid in front of them both, looking between them at an almost glacial pace. Emilia watched his chest rise and fall.

He had their absolute attention and it was utterly captivating and intensely arousing.

She squeezed her thighs together again as her breath caught in her chest.

Her heart seemed to skip a beat.

She was shaking with anticipation.

This was it, the moment she'd fantasised about for weeks.

He reached out both his hands, palms up, as the faintest

smile crossed his lips.

*

Cassian slipped his phone back into his pocket and looked up at the half moon. The waning crescent shimmered behind a thin blanket of mist, drifting low across the night sky. He took a deep breath and tried to calm down.

He couldn't help being turned on. Not after the conversation he'd just had.

The idea that his wife was a thousand miles away in a romantic villa south of the ancient city of Nimes, in the company of friends who might later this evening take her into their bed and make love to her. Make her orgasm. Cum inside her. All without him there by her side.

The idea was intensely arousing.

If someone had said to him six months ago that his wife would be having a threesome in a Villa in the south of France, and not only would he be okay with it, but he would be actively excited for her and turned on... he would have laughed.

And yet here he was now, picturing them together and wanting her to have an incredible time, wanting her to feel wanted and loved and cared for. To feel safe in their arms.

Perhaps that was what she was feeling too.

He had never been subtle about his attraction to Alice, but it had always been masked by jest. The truth was that he had been attracted to her since school. Not in the same way that he was attracted to Emilia, but he wasn't going to pretend that she wasn't beautiful, or radiant, or confident and funny, and sweet too, in her own often brutal way.

Whilst Emilia was innocent, Alice was anything but. He'd heard stories about her over the years, about her promiscuity and her propensity for enjoying more than one sexual partner at a time and this had only increased the allure she'd held.

But it wasn't just that. It wasn't even the sum total of *all* of that. There was a chemistry between them, and it was raw and powerful. At times it felt stretched to breaking point, as though despite everything, despite their mutual love for Emilia, they might have just snapped at any moment over the last ten years and fucked like wild animals.

Alice was his succubus and he was her incubus.

The more they tried to stay apart, the harder they wanted to tear each others clothes off, so they had found a balance over the years, without ever discussing it or accepting it or managing it.

And now that balance had tipped.

Emilia had given her *permission*, if that's what it was, for them to break their unspoken pact.

She'd meant it aswell.

This wasn't a joke like before. This wasn't banter or teasing, this wasn't her poking fun at her sister's inappropriate crush. She *wanted* them to do it.

Perhaps it was to make her feel better about what she wanted. A way of lessening any perceived guilt and assuaging her anxiety about what might constitute cheating.

But he wanted the three of them to be together, he wanted his wife to enjoy herself.

And she wanted him to enjoy himself too. But with her sister?

He could hear Alice moving around upstairs, then a moment later the light in their bedroom flicked off.

He took a deep breath and focused on calming his arousal and after a few moments his body began to follow orders and stand down. He couldn't go back inside trying to hide a hard-on.

He closed his eyes, his stomach full of butterflies, and then he flexed his fingers, turned around, and headed toward the back door, opening it up and stepped back into the warmth. For a moment, he stood still in the kitchen, clenching and unclenching his fingers as he listened to her making her way down the stairs. He eyed the bottle of wine he'd started earlier and considered pouring himself another glass for courage. A large one. He listened as she paused for a brief moment in the corridor and then made her way through to the lounge.

'Cass?' she called.

'I'm in here.'

'Do you have any wine?'

He grinned and reached for the bottle, hesitating as he went to pluck a second glass out of the illuminated shelf above the work surface.

'Big glass or small glass?'

'Small,' she said.

He nodded and took one down, pouring a measure of white into it until it was a fingers width from the top, then he filled his own and walked on through.

Alice was sat on the couch with her bare legs tucked underneath her, wearing nothing but one of Emilia's large baggy jumpers. Her hair was loose around her neck. It was shorter than her sisters and naturally wavy, and it was still a little damp from the shower.

She looked breathtaking.

She always did. When she smiled, Cassian felt his chest throb.

He proffered the wine glass and she accepted it gracefully, the tips of her fingers brushing gently against his and lingering for a moment longer than necessary.

He watched, almost frozen to the spot as she glanced down into the swirling liquid, closed her eyes and breathed in the heady aroma.

After a moments hesitation, he sat down opposite her in

the little armchair and took a small sip from his own glass, feeling his muscles relax as the fruity flavour washed across his taste buds.

For a while they sat together in silence, occasionally glancing at each other and smiling awkwardly, until Alice spoke.

'Do you love her?' she said suddenly, without looking up.

'Of course I do,' he said. 'More than anything.'

She nodded, pensive.

'I do too,' she swirled her wine gently around and around, staring into the little whirlpool. 'You know when we were little, she had a lisp? She used to call me *Alith.*'

He frowned. He didn't know that. Emilia had never told him. Alice nodded and continued.

'I'd be in my room, reading or playing dolls and she'd come rushing in asking me if she could play with me. *Alith! Alith!* She always wanted to be around me. At the time I found it annoying. I had this cuter, funnier, wide-eyed little copy of me blasting around behind me all the time, wanting to do everything I was doing. I had to share everything, because I was older than her. Dad would shout up the stairs - *She just wants to play, share it with her!* - as I was telling her off for playing with my favourite toy or drawing in my newest magazine. I was always afraid she'd damage them or never give them back. But she always did, she was so conscientious and gentle. It drove me mad. It was like living with a better, younger, prettier version of yourself.'

She took another sip of wine and looked back up at him before continuing.

'So I always used to tease her about her lisp. In my head, it was the one thing that I could do that she couldn't. I used to wind her up that she could never have a boyfriend called *Theve* or *Thamuel* or *Thilath*, because they wouldn't know who she was talking to. Of course she ended up with a *Catthian* and proved me wrong.'

He laughed and sipped his wine, listening intently.

'The infuriating thing was, whenever I used to tease her, she would just smile and laugh. It didn't get to her, my words didn't hurt her. They *couldn't* hurt her, because she loved me and for some reason, she looked up to me. At first it made me more and more angry, I couldn't even lash out at this perfect little mini-me. But the older I got, the more I matured, the more I understood what it was. She really *loved* me. She looked up to me, and saw me in a way that others didn't. She didn't see a stereotype of a nerd or a gangly tall girl, she didn't even see what I wanted people to see. She saw me for who I was and she wanted more than anything, for me to be happy.'

Alice stopped and pursed her lips, frowning. Then she took a deep breath and exhaled, looking into his eyes as she spoke.

'I wonder sometimes, if she wanted you, because *I* wanted you.'

Cassian frowned.

'And I don't mean that in a jealous way. I think she saw that I perceived value in you, and it opened her eyes to that value too.'

'You wanted me?'

Alice nodded and for the first time in almost a decade, she blushed. 'So *fucking* bad, I used to fantasise about you bending me over the tables at college, pushing my dress up, pulling my knickers aside and just fucking *taking* me.'

Cassian's hand started to shake as he licked his lips, his chest pounding as he tried to hold back a grin.

'Em's doing what she's always done. Looking after me, and now you. Making sure that we're happy.'

She tilted her head and smiled knowingly at Cassian. He watched as her tongue flicked out and delicately dabbed her lower lip.

'So that's why I asked if you love her. Because *I* love her, and I know she loves me and I need to know *you* love her. *Really* love her. Because if you don't, then-'

'Alice,' said Cassian, interrupting her. 'I love her.'

He smiled warmly, assured and confident. His love for his wife was one thing he could always be certain of, it was never in doubt.

Alice looked into his eyes and he met her gaze, tingling as neither one so much as blinked. After a while she grinned and looked down, laughing a little.

'If we do this, you have to understand that this is just sex. Nothing more, nothing less. This is us giving in to an *overwhelmingly fucking strong* urge. There's no feelings. I just want your cock inside me. You love her, I love her.'

For a while Cassian continued to stare at her, his heart racing, his chest pounding, running his eyes across her face, along her bare legs, over the curve of her hip, just barely outlined in the thick jumper that lay loose over her lithe frame. Then he stood up, never taking his eyes off her and walked over to the sofa. After a moment he reached out his hand and waited.

Alice looked up at him, smiling and then she slipped her long slender fingers inside his palm and stood up. He turned slowly, and led her out of the lounge, the long thick jumper falling down around her thighs, as her bare feet padded softly across the carpet.

He reached the bottom of the stairs and pulled her toward him, but to his surprise, she gently pulled back.

He turned around and she slipped her fingers out of his grasp, a sad smile on her face.

'I don't know if this is what I want,' she said quietly.

Cassian looked back at her, at her heartbroken expression, at her shining eyes, glistening in the moonlight bouncing down the hallway from the kitchen.

'We shouldn't do this,' she said. 'We can't go back from this. Em may think she's okay with this now, but what if she isn't?'

Cassian smiled warmly and nodded, reluctantly. 'You're right,' he said.

'What if she's just saying that it's okay because she doesn't want you to say she can't fuck Amy and Mark tonight?'

'I want that for her though, I don't want it to be an exchange. I meant it when I told her it was okay for them to be together.'

'She asked you?'

Cassian nodded.

'And you said yes?'

'Yeah.'

Alice took a deep breath. 'I love her so much, I don't want to ruin what you have.'

'You couldn't.'

Alice looked at him long and hard as she shook her head. After a while she closed her eyes and folded her arms, her head dropping down. Then she took a long deep breath. 'Fuck, I want you.'

Cassian looked down and smiled, shaking his head. 'You're right though.'

'No I'm not,' she said suddenly. 'If you want me, *tell* me you want me.'

He looked up and frowned, thinking. His mind was racing, conflicting feelings clashing in a whirlpool of lust and loyalty. Then his mouth took over. 'I want you.'

'Tell me you want to fuck me.'

Cassian could feel himself getting hard as he stared at her, his mouth open as her eyes pierced him with a burning passion.

'Tell me you want to bend me over and *fuck me* on the

dining room table.'

'I do,' he said. As he took a step down towards her she stepped away, still facing him.

'Tell me you want to make me cum.'

'I want to make you cum.'

'Tell me you want to fill me up.'

She took another step backward but Cassian was too fast. He grabbed hold of her by the waist and pushed her up against the wall of the corridor and suddenly her lips were pressed against his and her hands were undoing his belt.

He thrust himself against her and she moaned into his cheek as she felt how hard he was, and as his buckle came loose she unzipped his fly and reached inside for his cock.

'She always told me it was big,' she said as she bit down softly on his lower lip and grinned.

Cassian picked her up and she wrapped her bare legs around his waist as he stepped out of his jeans and carried her easily over to the dining room table. He sat her down on the shiny surface as she wrapped her hands around his back and squeezed her body against him.

'I want you inside me,' she gasped as he pulled at her jumper, lifting it up and over her head, exposing her bare chest. He pulled her towards him with one hand and kissed her hard, moaning as his other hand caressed her breast.

She breathed into his chest and then he stepped back, pulling her with him and sliding her down until her feet touched the floor, where she stood almost naked before him, grinning and nervous.

She took a deep breath and exhaled, shaking as the two of them looked into each others eyes with unconcealed lust. Years of restraint unravelling in seconds as they finally gave in to their long repressed lust.

With one strong hand he turned her around and pushed her forward until she was flat and bent over on the table, her arms outstretched either side of her.

Then slowly he spread her legs apart with his foot.

'Yes, do it,' she said. 'Fuck me.'

In two quick movements, Cassian slipped his own boxers off, letting them fall to the floor and then he pulled her knickers down around her ankles. She wriggled in arousal, desperate for him as he pinned her down with one arm, his other hand resting against her bottom.

She was bare in front of him.

Dripping and desperate.

She sensed him lining up.

This was it.

She closed her eyes.

And held her breath.

*

Emilia tried to stop herself from giggling as Mark led her and Amy by the hand into their bedroom. Together they walked slowly up to the side of their enormous king size bed and stopped, smiling and stealing glances at one other awkwardly. Amy squeezed her hand and turned her a little to face her as Mark stood behind her, holding her hips, his breath a gentle breeze on the back of her neck.

'Is this okay?' said Amy, looking into her eyes as she stood before her, sandwiched delicately between them.

Emilia nodded urgently, her breathing shallow and fast. She had wanted this so much and had thought about it for so long, but now it was happening it was almost too much. Her whole body was shaking with desire. She wanted to be shared by them and to be with them, to feel close and warm and loved by them.

She bit her lip and smiled as she felt Mark's fingers run underneath the edge of her top at the same time as Amy took one intimate step closer.

Together, with Emilia pressed between them, they slowly pulled her loose camisole up and over her head. As it came free, Amy leaned in and kissed her neck, the palm of her left hand against her cheek, her other hand hurriedly undoing her little black belt.

At the same time, Emilia began to pull at Amy's colourful summer dress, unbuttoning it at the front and giggling as she felt Mark's cock grow and press hard against the back of her thighs.

He began kissing her neck, softly at first and then harder, his fingers slipping down between the now loose gap around her waist as Amy unbuttoned her skin-tight jeans.

The three of them shifted back and forth like a wave in the middle of the ocean, smooth but powerful as they kissed and caressed one another, moving as one.

It felt natural and easy, as though it was always meant to be this way.

As Emilia undid the last button, Amy's dress slipped away over her shoulders and down around her ankles where she almost tripped, stumbling forward into her and Mark who kept them all upright as they laughed.

'You okay?' whispered Emilia as Amy blushed and nodded.

She turned around now and Mark leaned in to kiss her lips as Amy tugged at her jeans from behind, pulling them down urgently over her bottom and onto the floor, and then pressing her almost naked body against the curve of her back as she reached around to help her girlfriend undo her husband's trousers.

It felt so naughty, touching another man without her own husband present, and in so many other ways it felt so good.

Emilia fumbled with his fly as Amy's fingers joined her and together they pulled them down around his waist, his boxers coming with them, exposing his magnificent and throbbing cock. They smiled in unison as it surged with excitement.

Mark stepped aside and then unbuttoned his own shirt, looking the two girls in front of him up and down with such a powerful lust that Amy faltered and took a step back.

He nodded toward the bed, commanding them to sit back as he stood, admiring their forms as they lay down together. He stalked around the side slowly as they watched with anticipation and when he reached the end he kneeled down, moved up between their thighs, and reached out for Emilia's knickers.

~

Cassian pushed forward, pressing just the tip of his member against Alice's lips, teasing her softly. He knew she wanted him to fuck her, but he wasn't ready yet. He wanted to savour this, the sight of her, the sensations, how wet she felt.

He smiled, his fingers running across her smooth bottom as he slid himself up and down. Then Alice felt herself opening up and she moaned.

Her fingers splayed out across the shiny surface of the table as she closed her eyes, her mouth opening wide as her sisters husband entered her for the first time in her life.

She'd wanted this for years. Wanted *him*. And now it was finally happening.

As he pushed inside he slowed right down, leisurely filling her up with his cock until she couldn't take him in any further. Keeping still, not breathing, his eyes closed.

She could feel him throbbing inside her and she felt full. He felt better inside of her than any other man that had come before and it was dizzying. Perhaps it was how close they were, perhaps it was how taboo this was. Either way, it felt *incredible.*

Cassian remained still, savouring the sensation, the warmth, the tightness. She seemed to squeeze and relax around him like a wave, running up and down his length as though she was feeling and sensing every inch of him.

Then he pulled back, and thrust and she cried out in pleasure.

~

Amy kneeled up in front of Mark's manhood as Emilia looked up at him in awe. He looked like a statue of a Greek god. She had to stop herself from giggling as he gazed down at her as though he was a Roman Emperor and she was his little concubine for the night.

His firm jaw, his chiseled abs, his toned thighs and of course, his thick and proud cock. It was too much.

Amy took her hand and beckoned her to kneel beside him, then she turned and kissed her as Mark looked down on them both, running the palm of his hand up and down his length.

Amy's hand slid down Emilia's chest and her thumb brushed across her nipple, sending shivers down her spine, and then she pulled back, gasping for her and grinning, glancing sideways with mischief in her eyes at Mark.

Emilia smiled and nodded and the two of them turned and shuffled closer to him, until his cock was between each of their mouths and then they leaned forward and began to kiss him. Just little pecks at first, starting at the base and slowly making their way up his shaft as he closed his eyes and relaxed.

Amy's lips met Emilia's at the tip and Mark's knees buckled as the girls kissed, their tongues rolling across his glans as Amy began to pump him with her hand. As his wife pulled away, Emilia eagerly took him into her mouth and slid him across her tongue, tasting him and feeling him strain and pulse. Then she slid back and Amy took her place, taking him as far as she could into the back of her throat.

Mark took Emilia's hand on one side and Amy's on the other as they continued to fellate him, his cock twitching as he got closer and closer. Then suddenly he pulled back unable to take it any longer. He lowered himself and kissed them both, then lay Emilia backwards until she was flat, Amy by her side as Mark parted her thighs.

As she lay back she thought of Cassian and Alice and whether they were together right now back home and she smiled.

~

'Harder,' said Alice as Cassian's length plunged into her warmth.

She felt deeper than Emilia, and he found he could let loose more without hurting her, so he obeyed, thrusting as he held her down, keeping her in place.

'Yes, *fuck*,' moaned Alice, her cheek pressed flat against the cold wooden table.

He was strong, and she liked that. She liked how it felt to be pinned down with his one arm, unable to move as he had his way with her. She could feel herself getting wetter and wetter as she reached out for the far edge of the table so she could brace herself better against his thrusts.

'Hit me,' she said.

Cassian's palm smacked against her tight little bottom, the noise echoing in the large space of the lounge diner.

'Again,' she pleaded.

Smack.

'*Put your finger in my ass,*' she begged, biting her lip in anticipation.

Cassian traced his thumb down between her cheeks, teasing her until it was pressing against her cute little button.

Then he pushed.

Alice moaned deeply into the table as the sensation flowed over her. His huge cock in her pussy, his thumb inside her ass.

He didn't slow down, continuing to pound her at the same steady pace, pressing his thumb deeper and deeper into her.

Then suddenly he was pulling her backwards and upright to standing as he continued to fuck her, kissing her neck as she wrapped her arm around the back of his head. She felt his palm cup her breast and squeeze her nipple as his cock slipped out of her, then he spun her around.

For a moment they stared at one another again, a powerful and passionate lust in their eyes and then Cassian picked her up, pulling her thighs up and sliding them around his waist.

~

Amy reached down and slipped her fingers around Mark's cock and Emilia watched as she guided him toward her, the anticipation of his touch against her pussy was almost too much to bear and she closed her eyes and breathed in.

Cassian wasn't here, and everything felt so *naughty*.

Another man - another woman's husband - was about to push inside of her and make love to her, and her own husband was a thousand miles away, alone with her sister.

Her whole body tensed and strained as she waited and just as she felt she was about to burst, his skin touched hers and she shook and gasped, exhaling as his thick member slipped into her pussy and for a moment, she pictured Cassian and felt a pang of guilt.

Amy leaned up and kissed her hard on the lips, distracting

her and then she felt her girl's fingers slide between her legs as Mark's cock slipped in and out of her, pressing between her parting and then circling her clit.

She sighed into Amy's mouth, one hand on the back of her girlfriend's head as she fumbled for Mark's fingers, clasping her hand around them and squeezing them tight as he gently thrust himself, a deep rumbling moan escaping his lips.

His thick cock felt so good, filling her insides so completely with each push. As Amy pulled away Emilia looked up at him and saw that his free hand was between his wife's legs, his fingers inside her, deftly pleasuring her.

He leaned back as Amy looked his way too, and then he smiled as she tucked her legs beneath her and knelt up. Emilia watched with growing excitement as the curvy little redhead lifted her leg and straddled her chest and then began to kiss her husbands lips, her sweet little entrance glistening and sparkling just inches above her face.

Emilia placed her hands either side of Amy's thighs and guided her backwards as she lowered herself. Then she tilted her head back and ran her tongue along her bare and sweet parting, tasting and savouring her as she quivered and wiggled.

She moaned as Emilia's lips pressed into her, making Mark quicken his pace as he kissed his wife, pulling her towards him as he made love to the girl spread between her thighs. Emilia's body arched as he pleasured her, pushing deeper into Amy with her tongue, her soaking wet parting tasting sweet against her lips as she rocked back and forth.

Then suddenly Amy was turning around and sliding down, straddling Emilia's waist and learning forward until their breasts were touching and pressed together, their hard nipples slipping against one another. Their lips met as Mark pulled out of her and a moment later Amy was thrust forward, moaning into Emilia's pussy soaked mouth as the muscle bound Greek god penetrated his own wife.

His goddess.

Her goddess.

Emilia squirmed as Amy's fingers found her clit and began to circle it, faster and faster as Mark thrust harder and harder, making her cry out in pleasure as he grew.

Then suddenly he was back inside her again, taking her by surprise as his slick cock parted her lips and slid deep. She squeezed down on him and smiled as he moaned, his cock twitching like all the times before. She could tell he was getting close.

She wanted him to cum inside her, to fill her up like he had more than once now. She wanted to know she could satisfy him, to feel good and wanted and loved by him.

She almost cried out *No!* as he pulled out of her again and slid back into Amy, her body writhing in protest, her pussy feeling incomplete once more.

~

Cassian carried Alice towards the wall as they kissed, pinning her up and holding her there, suspended in his arms as his rock solid cock found her opening again and glided inside easily, pumping into her as he pressed his head between her breasts and wrapped his lips around her nipple.

Alice grabbed his hair and held it tight as she cried out in ecstasy at the sensation. It was all so wrong and yet it felt so right.

She was going to cum, and she was going to cum *hard*.

She started to grind against him as her orgasm built, writhing up and down, rubbing her clit against his body as his tongue swept around her nipple and his cock plunged in and of her, bucking her up and down against the wall.

She dug her nails into his back as she climaxed and threw

her head back as she gushed over the edge, her whole body throbbing with desire and lust as Cassian kept going, harder and harder.

Then a moment later, she felt him erupt. She had come just before him, her pussy squeezing him and milking him and now she could feel him sticky and warm and sweet.

Each throb as he spilled inside her felt raw and urgent, each pulse and surge stretching her as his body strained. The way his abs tightened and his thighs became rock solid as he shot inside her made her cum harder, her orgasm rolling into another as rope after rope of warmth filled her up.

~

Emilia heard Mark take a deep breath, and looked up to see his eyes closed and his pace quicken. She reached between Amy's legs and began to slide her finger up and down her clit as Mark began to lose control.

She smiled as she thought about how overwhelming it must be for him, watching them kiss, watching them make love as he fucked either of them at will, not having to share with Cassian, not having to worry about envy, just the love and worship of his two beautiful women.

Amy's head arched back as he moaned and came, pumping her with his seed, and Emilia watched her mouth as it widened, reaching up to caress her girlfriend's breast.

Then her own eyes widened as suddenly and to her surprise, she felt Mark's still hard cock pushing back into her and a moment later she felt a shot of his warmth, spurting inside her as he strained and moaned.

She grinned at Amy in shock, who was now looking down as they realised he'd managed to cum inside *both* of them.

She could still feel him going, her thighs felt sticky and so did her tummy and she realised that Amy was dripping with his love and it was settling on her and pooling into her belly button, warm and sweet.

It was incredible.

And it was *so* rude.

'I love you,' she said to Amy as she kissed her again, giggling with pleasure.

'I love you too.'

~

As Alice's body slumped onto Cassian's shoulders, he turned and carried her onto the couch, laying her down on her back gently as she recovered. Then he lay down beside her and wrapped his arm over the top of her naked body, cradling her protectively and making her feel warm and safe.

Her heart was pounding in her chest and her ears felt like they were ringing. For the first time in a long time, she felt different. Despite the situation, despite their relationship, there was no feeling of regret. No feeling of shame or embarrassment.

She was just happy, and for a while she simply basked in that emotion, letting it warm and envelop her, like his big arms around her chest.

'Are you alright?' he said after some time.

She nodded and turned to face him, wriggling around and then tucking her arms up, holding his face in her palms.

'I am,' she said, nodding with a beaming smile. 'Are you?'

'I just fucked my wife's hot sister, so yes.'

Alice laughed shyly and then kissed him long and hard.

He could feel her shaking as she drew a deep breath, and then she whispered. 'Wanna go upstairs and do it again?'

*

CHAPTER THREE

Emilia blinked in the bright morning sun, shining in through the open shutters as she woke up with her head nestled comfortably between Amy's breasts. The beautiful redhead's eyes were still closed, a faint smile adorning her lips as she breathed in and out softly, tickling the loose strands of hair around Emilia's ears.

She could hear Mark moving around down the corridor and she couldn't decide if she could smell croissants or pancakes cooking. Either way she felt immediately hungry.

It was blissful.

She stroked her fingers slowly across Amy's smooth skin and crested the round of her bare breast with her palm, brushing her curves with her thumb as she thought about last night and stifled a giddy laugh.

Then her mind wandered back further to her conversation with Cassian and Alice.

Had they made love? She wondered.

Would they have gone that far?

Her phone was on the side table. She hadn't heard it go off, but she didn't want to reach out for it to check and risk disturbing Amy.

Perhaps they hadn't woken up yet? Or perhaps they were doing it *again?*

She laughed at the thought and turned gently to look up at the still and sleeping girl beneath her.

Could this really work?

Their marital status had gone from *Married* to *It's Complicated* in a matter of weeks, and now it was positively *WTF*. She was starting to think she might need to create a schedule for their relationship to avoid conflicts and she was half way through wondering if there was an app for that when Amy started to stir.

'Mmm,' she moaned happily as she opened her eyes, reaching her hand out to stroke her girlfriend's long blonde hair.

'I'm sorry,' said Emilia. 'I think I dribbled on your boobs.'

Amy laughed as she rubbed her eyes with her other hand. 'What time is it?'

'Early. We've got to leave in a bit to go get Cass.'

'As much as I love your husband, I could so go for another two to three hours in bed.'

Amy looked bleary-eyed out the window at the blue skies and the gently swaying palm trees, then she looked down at Emilia and frowned. 'Have you heard from them?'

'I don't know, I didn't want to wake you,' she nodded to where her phone lay, face down on the little side table.

Amy reached across and picked it up, shielding her eyes so as not to see the screen as she handed it down.

Emilia took it and saw one unread message from Cassian. It was from late last night.

Night, night, beautiful. I hope you all had an amazing night. I love you, you are the best xxx

Emilia shrugged. 'It just says goodnight,' she laughed. 'He's keeping me in suspense, clearly.'

'Do you *want* to know?'

Mark knocked on the open door as Emilia began to answer, dressed in nothing but a pinafore and holding a tray of coffee, cranberry juice, croissants and what looked like a freshly cut baguette with a clove of butter on the side.

'Oh my goodness,' said Amy, sitting up excited as Emilia rolled aside. 'This looks amazing.'

Emilia slid up the bed until she was upright against the headboard, shoulder to shoulder with Amy. She smiled widely at both the naked man-waiter in the pinafore and the continental breakfast-in-bed that had been laid out before them.

'Thank you,' she said as she reached out for a croissant, taking a delicate bite as the sweet pastry crumbled against her lips.

'How did you girls sleep?'

Emilia nodded enthusiastically and then mimed fainting.

'You did yourself proud,' laughed Amy. 'We both passed out.'

Mark nodded slowly, satisfied and grinning with pride.

'Last night was amazing,' said Emilia quietly, having swallowed her bite. 'Thank you.'

'Anytime,' said Amy, raising her eyebrows suggestively and looking between them.

'As much as I'd love a repeat performance this morning,' said Mark. 'We *do* need to leave in forty five minutes to go and get Cass.'

Amy rolled her eyes disappointedly and grinned.

'Wait, forty five minutes from *now?*' she said, her expression changing in a flash.

Mark nodded, nabbing the end piece of the baguette.

Amy wriggled out of the bed and hopped down onto the tiled floor in her bare feet.

'Why didn't you wake me earlier?' she said, skittering towards the en-suite. 'I'm never going to be ready in time.'

Emilia laughed as Amy shut the door and then a moment later she opened it again, peering out in alarm.

'Em, can you choose me something to wear?'

She laughed harder, her mouth full of croissant, nodding as she tried to stop herself spraying pastry over Mark, who was shaking his head.

'You don't need as much time to get ready?' he asked.

Emilia shook her head, swallowing her mouthful and taking a breath.

'Yes but this is too much fun to watch,' she laughed, her little frame bouncing up and down. 'But no, seriously, we're going to be late.'

She burst out laughing again as Amy came running out once more to grab her towel in a wild panic, and then disappeared back into the en-suite, slamming the door.

'Don't worry,' said Mark, finishing up the last piece of croissant. 'I'll get us there on time.'

*

Alice woke up from a deep and gentle slumber, feeling more fully rested and recharged than she'd felt in years. She allowed herself a moment of blissful happiness, recalling how incredible everything had felt last night, before opening the trapdoor holding back the existential dread that was festering deep inside of her as a result of her recent employment predicament, her homelessness and the fact that after years of joking about it she had finally fucked her sister's husband.

One problem at a time.

She'd been fired.

Sort of.

That was the easiest way to explain it to Emilia in any case, and there was no way she was going to start explaining everything in more detail to her beloved sister right now. The poor girl was riddled with anxiety and the last thing she needed to know was exactly what had happened yesterday.

That would involve explaining *exactly* what she did for a living.

And that was not a conversation she was prepared to have right now.

Perhaps ever.

She heard Cassian's footsteps coming up the stairs.

Her natural instinct for dignity kicked in and she covered herself up, tucking the duvet up to her chin.

Then she laughed at herself, and the absurdity of the whole situation. Here she was, naked in her sisters bed, having had the best sex of her life last night with her sisters husband.

'Oh *fuck*,' she said, sighing under her breath as she waited for him to walk through the door. She felt like a schoolgirl again.

He would be leaving soon. Flying down to the south of France to join his wife and their swinger friends for just under a week of fun in the sun.

She wanted to be going with them, but that wasn't right or fair. Not now.

She had to get her life in order first. That was her priority.

The best sex of her *life*, though. It really had been, without a doubt. She'd never had an orgasm like it.

Rolling, multiple and toe curling.

She'd cried out so loud she was afraid the neighbours would call the police.

She'd felt utterly and completely satisfied, and desperate for more.

Cassian was something else.

He pushed open the door slowly, peering inside and found her smiling at him from behind her duvet shield.

'Hey,' she said, quietly.

'Morning.'

'Are you off?'

'Soon.'

She smiled at him and took a deep breath. He walked over and she tucked her knees up so he could sit down on the bed in front of her.

He looked at her and smiled and she tingled as his eyes made their way slowly over her face, looking at her eyes, her mouth, her nose. She felt giddy and she couldn't help but smile. It was as though he'd wanted to gaze on her for so long but couldn't, but now things had changed, he was taking his time, savouring her, drinking her in.

He looked down, smiling and then glanced back sideways.

'What you said last night,' he spoke slowly. 'When you asked me if I loved her? If I'd said no, would you-'

'Have walked out? Yes.' Cassian smiled as she continued. 'If you didn't truly love her? If there was some niggling doubt in your mind, that somehow the grass might be greener with me and that you could jump ship and switch to the older sister mid-game? I'd have walked away, and never looked back,' she smiled, and then leaned forward, taking his hand in hers. 'Attraction isn't cheating, Cass. Lust isn't cheating. *Sex* isn't cheating. Dishonesty is cheating. No one is being dishonest.' She breathed in and huffed, then leaned back against the headboard. 'Marriage and monogamy are imagined orders, they're .'

'That sounds like a quote.'

'Go ahead and fucking quote me then,' she laughed.

'Is this wrong?'

'Have we lied? No. I've never pretended to you or Em that I don't fancy you or that I don't want to fuck you. It's only wrong because our culture has decided it's wrong. There's nothing objectively wrong with sex for pleasure with whoever we want. It's the cultural order that we've created that tells us it's taboo. That forbids us to sleep with our neighbours wife, or… our sisters husband.'

'You've been thinking about this?'

She shrugged and looked down into her lap. 'For years,' she laughed. 'It might be deemed wrong by others, but it felt right to me.'

'Me too,' he smiled and squeezed her fingers.

'I think Em gets it too. At least I bloody hope she does.'

Cassian laughed, but he felt strange. He couldn't shake the creeping feeling of guilt. As though this had been a test that he'd failed.

Emilia wasn't like that though, she was honest, she didn't play games or trick him. She was amazing. Innocent in her own way, and pure.

Somehow that made him feel worse.

'I think she gets it more than we do,' he said, smiling. 'Well, more than I do at least.'

'Do you need to go?'

He nodded.

'Shame, I was hoping for round three.'

'Rain check?'

'Deal.'

'You got everything you need?'

Alice shrugged. 'Oh, wait. Em said I could guess the code to your safe?' she frowned, confused.

Cassian grinned as he stood up, nodding. 'Did she now?'

'Any clues?'

'It won't take you long to figure out.'

Alice stared blankly at him and then after second or two of thought, she smiled and nodded.

'I think I know.'

She slipped her bare legs out the side of the bed and pushed the covers aside, smiling at Cassian as she stood up naked in front of him, and then leaned in for a hug.

He hesitated, frozen in surprise and then wrapped his arms around her bare torso, pulling her in tight.

'Thank you,' she whispered in his ear, making the hairs on his neck stand on end. 'Sure you don't want to stay for round three? You could fuck my ass?'

Cassian closed his eyes, almost dizzy with sudden arousal. He took a deep breath and exhaled through pursed lips.

'If I don't leave now, I'll miss my plane.'

Alice laughed. 'Go,' she said, pushing him away and turning him around. 'Be with her, be with them. Give her my love.'

Cassian walked to the door and turned back, looking her up and down and shaking his head.

'Stay safe, Alice. Call us if you need anything.'

'I will.'

She winked as he shut the door, listening as he went down the stairs; the front door closing, the key in the lock, the car starting and reversing out onto the road. She huffed and turned to look at herself in the free standing mirror, admiring the shape of her body, the imperfections, the curves, the bumps.

After a while she turned and pulled open the cupboard door and knelt down to look more closely at the little safe. It had a red light next to a little keypad. She reached toward it and pressed the first button, then she tapped the next five numbers in quick succession.

The light went green.

'Em, you little bitch.'

It was set to her date of birth.

'I fucking love you,' she laughed as she looked at the small pile of cash inside.

* * *
*

The airport was heaving with passengers and tourists as the trio made their way into the arrivals area. The drive had been as smooth and as fast as on the way out, but this time Emilia had felt a little more relaxed and safe. She'd sat up front with Mark whilst Amy had snoozed in the back and had found the experience surprisingly exciting and more than a little arousing.

By the time they'd arrived at the airport she'd decided she would be buying Cassian a racing car experience day for his birthday and booking a hotel for later that night.

She looked up at the arrivals board, searching for the flight number and the airport listing. Amy pointed up as she saw it flicker past.

'There,' she said. 'AF1691. Landed ten minutes ago. He should be off the plane soon.'

Emilia smiled and did her best not to jump up and down on the spot. She'd missed him dearly, even it had only been for a couple of days. She wanted to hear his voice again and see his face. To kiss him and to hold him.

'I'll go get some coffees,' said Mark.

'Oh, could I have a decaf?' she said quickly, touching his arm and smiling.

'Me too,' said Amy as Mark nodded and peeled off toward a busy cafe situated on the concourse. A tannoy sounded through the hangar like space and a man spoke quickly in French and then again in accented English.

'Please do not leave baggage unattended-'.

Amy tuned out the noise and turned to Emilia, reaching for her hand and squeezing it.

'You okay?' she said.

She took her eyes away from the exit tunnel and nodded.

'Isn't it better that you don't know?'

Emilia shrugged. 'I don't think it matters. I'll always love them both, who I am to tell them what they cant and can't do with their bodies?'

Amy shook her head, smiling in awe at her girlfriend. 'I think you and the Dalai Lama would get along very well.'

Emilia laughed, but the truth was, she was conflicted. Last night everything had made sense but this morning she had been struggling to rationalise it. In her excitement and anticipation of spending the night with Mark and Amy, she had felt guilty about Cassian's absence, and in her eagerness to please him, and her almost compulsive need to make her sister happy, she had not just agreed but actually seeded the idea of something that she was no longer sure she was comfortable with, and she had no one to blame but herself.

She hadn't wanted to disappoint Amy or Mark, and she didn't want to let Cassian down either. She had been so busy trying to make sure that everyone else was happy, that she hadn't realised that she was actually being selfish.

When she'd woken up this morning there was a part of her that had hoped to see a message from Cassian saying that he and Alice had slept apart and that he was looking forward to seeing her today.

Every now and again she would regain the rationality and composure she'd had last night. That strange and unconventional part of her that was not only *okay* with what might have happened between them, but was positively *encouraging* it. It felt like the elusive feather that Amy had described some weeks back, that sense of enlightenment, of purity and emotional maturity, understanding and compassion.

She took a deep breath.

No matter what had happened, she would forgive him.

No. *Forgive* was the wrong word.

There was nothing to forgive. She had consented.

But she would move past it. She hoped. She would have to, it wouldn't be fair on Mark and Amy to join them on their holiday and then ruin it with drama and upset.

She took a deep breath and turned back to the board. As she scanned it for Cassian's flight her phone buzzed in the back pocket of her shorts. She reached around and pulled it out, expecting to see a message from Cassian letting her know he was waiting for his luggage or off the plane, but instead it was Alice.

She froze.

Cassian was a gentleman. He wouldn't kiss and tell. But Alice was as blunt as a sledgehammer.

Fuck, fuck, fuck.

She had to read it, but it couldn't have come at a worse time.

She swiped.

Amy, still staring up the board, glanced sideways at the flurry of movement and saw a frown cross Emilia's face as she began to read.

Shitting fuck Em. Your husband just got promoted from The Greek to The Greek GOD. His cock is like a magic fucking wand. I've never come that hard in my life. TWICE. You get this every NIGHT? We are doing this again. P.S. I love you so much, you are the best sister in the whole world and I will never stop loving you. P.P.S. You remember saying this was okay right? RIGHT? If not, this whole text is bullshit and I'm just talking bollocks. I stayed at Mum's and we watched the Antiques Roadshow. It was shit xXx

She stared, open mouthed at the words before her, and then she started to laugh.

Amy glanced back again at the sound and looked at her,

confused and frowning.

'What is it? Is it Cass?'

'It's Alice,' said Emilia, shaking her head and giggling harder.

'What did she say?'

She was laughing so hard now that tears were running down her face. She handed the phone to Amy who scanned it and then stifled a laugh too.

'Oh my goodness, your sister is *nuts*.'

A flight of passengers were beginning to exit the arrival gates but it was too early to be Cassian's, and Emilia was now almost bent over and it was beginning to draw attention. Amy took her arm and guided her away to a row of nearby seats, sitting her down next to an elderly French lady reading a newspaper called *L'Humanite*.

'Are you okay?' Amy said, kneeling down in front of her.

Emilia's eyes were streaming with tears, but Amy could tell they were happy not sad.

'Yes,' she said, nodding emphatically. 'Is there something wrong with me?'

Amy shook her head slowly.

'I'm just really happy for them. But that's fucking *weird* right?'

The elderly lady looked sideways at them for a moment and then turned back to her paper.

'No, you're not weird. I think I get it. I love seeing you with Mark. When I see how happy you make him and how happy he makes you, it just fills me with this feeling of absolute joy. It's so powerful that it's almost addictive, I want to see more, to feel more and it's because I love you and you love me and they love us. With your sister, that bond is even stronger. You want her to be happy and you want Cassian to be happy and the idea of them making each other happy, physically or emotionally, makes you happy.'

Emilia nodded, and reached out her hands for Amy's who clasped them together tightly across her knees.

'I just, I love you all so much,' she said, laughing through her tears. 'But I don't want to be a doormat either.'

'No one thinks that. We love you.'

'But I should be *angry*, that's what I'm supposed to feel, *right?* My husband fucked my sister last night. Twice, apparently. And any minute now he's going to walk through *that* gate and I think I'm supposed to feel physically sick with jealously and rage but instead I'm so excited for them both that I've got butterflies in my stomach. What's wrong with me?'

'You want my advice?' said the lady next to them, leaning in with a thick American accent, surprising them both. 'Life's too short to spend it miserable. Find your own happiness, and then do whatever is in your power to make other people happy. That's all that matters. You kids sound like you got a good thing going on. Don't let other people tell you what should and shouldn't make you happy. Only you get to decide that.'

Emilia and Amy blinked at the woman, their mouths wide open.

'Thank you,' said Emilia after a moment.

'You're welcome, is that your husband?' the woman pointed behind them to where Cassian stood, suitcase in his hand, frowning in confusion.

They both stared and then a moment later they jumped up, running over towards him and wrapping their arms around him in their excitement. He lifted them up, one in each arm, embracing them tightly.

'Hey pal,' said Mark as he walked back over, carrying four coffee's on a small tray. 'Good to see you.'

Emilia kissed his face as he lowered her back down.

'*Alice told me,*' she whispered, grinning at him. 'It's okay.'

Cassian nodded and for a moment she thought she saw his eyes glisten and his throat bob as he took on what she'd said, but then it passed and he smiled with relief.

'How was your flight?' said Amy, stroking his hand in hers.

'Good, bit noisy, but smooth. There was a rowdy group of embarrassing Brits drinking heavily, but by the time we were halfway here they'd mostly passed out.'

'Is that them?' laughed Mark, pointing.

A group of around fifteen bedraggled and miserable looking men and women were stumbling their way out through the doors, swearing and arguing with one another.

'That's them.'

'Always a pleasure,' said Mark, handing Cassian one of the coffees from the tray. 'Milk and one sugar?'

He smiled and nodded. 'Thanks mate.'

'The villa is beautiful,' said Emilia, holding his hand as she tried not to jump up and down. 'You're going to love it.'

'She's right,' said Amy. 'It's our own little paradise.'

'Did you Christen it last night?'

Mark laughed, as Emilia looked down at the floor in shame.

'Fuck yes,' said Amy, holding up her hand for a high five from her husband, who nearly lost the balance of the coffee tray in doing so. 'Mark managed a two for one.'

Cassian looked confused and Amy stopped and whispered into his ear as his eyes widened.

'I think I have a lot to live up to,' he said, laughing.

'You better,' said Amy. 'If Alice has worn you out I'm gonna be pissed.'

Cassian looked stunned.

'Emilia told us,' she said. 'You cheeky fucker.'

'Shall we get cracking?' said Mark as Cassian looked on, grateful for the change of conversation. 'Maybe you can recharge your batteries on route?'

'Why?'

'Because we're all fucking in the pool when we get back,' said Amy, laughing and walking ahead of them as Emilia burst into laughter.

*

Emilia stood naked on the warm tiles of the en-suite bathroom, the door back into their bedroom open wide with her suitcase exploded in the centre of the bed. She'd brought three different swimming costumes with her and she was struggling to decide which one to wear.

When they'd nervously agreed to meet Amy and Mark at the Aurora Spa back in Oxford, she'd taken her one piece along and whilst it had a nostalgic value it wasn't the most flattering compared to Amy's stunning and simple two piece that she'd worn that day. She smiled as she thought back to how beautiful she'd looked, elegant and bold, full of confidence and passion, with just a touch of vulnerability. It had reminded her of the fifties pin up illustrations that she loved so much. Those voluptuous and curvy women, flaunting their sexuality, but still shy and human beneath their glossy veneer.

The one piece was flattering, but it seemed less *fun* than her white two piece string bikini. She stepped into the bottoms and drew them up to her waist, tying off one side into a neat little quick-release bow, as she struggled to stem the already rising feelings of arousal at the idea of the four of them swimming together in their own private pool.

She was still struggling with her emotions, but she was determined to put it all behind her now and focus on enjoying herself, not just for her sake but for all of them.

She picked up the bikini top and looped it over her head,

tying the back string tight and pressing her curvy breasts together at the same time. She looked at herself in the mirror and smiled as she tied her long, thick blonde hair into a quick ponytail.

She loved her body. It wasn't perfect, but it was hers and she loved herself. It was something their mum had said often when they were little. *The first person you should love is you.* She turned, twisting her waist as she looked herself up and down.

This was the right one.

The one-piece was too conservative for this afternoon. She wanted to *wow* Cassian and remind him of the woman he married. He may have fucked her sister last night, but he was going to make love with her today and that was all that mattered.

She also wanted Mark to untie her string and do her under the water of the pool as Cassian watched. Maybe both of her men at the same time again, like the first time they'd all been together.

She was getting too excited.

Her mind was like a rollercoaster.

One step at a time.

She took a deep breath and bundled all of her clothes back into her suitcase, closing the lid and sliding it off the bed and back onto the floor. Despite her fastidious organisation at home, when she was on holiday she didn't like to unpack, preferring instead to keep everything ready so she could leave at a moment's notice. She didn't really understand the compulsion, and presumed it was related to her anxiety, but she had long ago accepted it, not daring to look too close at the reasons, for fear of what she might find.

Standing up, she wrapped herself in a black lace sarong, and after another furtive glance in the mirror, she opened the door and stepped out onto the somewhat colder tiles of the corridor that ran through the centre of the villa.

She quickly found Cassian and Mark sharing a beer in the kitchen and as she walked in, she flicked her hair and swung her hips, enjoying the faces of both men as they were silenced by her entrance.

'Hey,' she said.

Mark coughed and then laughed, exhaling. 'Hey, you look, erm...'

'Like a Bond girl,' finished Cassian, sipping his beer straight from the bottle.

She smiled and raised her eyebrows. 'Thank you. Where's Amy?'

'Still getting ready,' said Mark, grinning.

As soon as he spoke, Emilia heard a door close and Amy stepped in behind her a moment later.

She was struggling to take her eyes off the men, their abs and muscles on show, dressed only in their black swimming shorts, but she peeled her eyes away to glance sideways and grinned as she saw a flash of red.

Amy was wearing a new bikini. It was flame coloured, with a gold ring that connected the separate triangles of her top, leaving a tantalising amount of cleavage on display which she couldn't help looking at.

She looked stunning.

'Shall we?' she said, tipping her head sideways and then walking out of the room, followed by Emilia as the men's eyes dropped.

Cassian downed his beer and almost slammed it onto the marble surface of the kitchen counter, then nodded, clapping his hands together as Mark grinned and winked, following them out.

The pool was almost cold as Emilia made her way down the steps and into the rippling, glistening water. She held tight onto Amy's hand as it rose up closer and closer to her bikini bottom, making her feel dizzy and giddy, then as it became too much she let go and swam forward, submerging herself and pushing off into a gentle breast stroke toward the deep end. A moment later she heard Amy scream and then do the same, splashing behind her as she followed her in up to her neck.

As she reached the far end, she turned and rested against the side, embracing the little redhead as she drew near and kissing her softly on the lips.

'It's colder than it looks,' she said, laughing as they held each other and floated in a slow circle.

Amy was about to respond when they heard running feet followed by the shadows of the two men leaping over their heads and crashing into the water, unleashing a tidal wave which splashed over and soaked the pair of them.

Cassian emerged first, slicking his hair back and wiping his eyes as he tread water, laughing and smiling at the shocked faces of his wife and her girlfriend. Mark emerged a few seconds later at the far end, having swum beneath the surface like a manta ray, gliding along the bottom of the pool before emerging into the sun, glistening with water droplets that seemed to roll off his skin in slow motion.

'*Fuck me*,' Emilia whispered under her breath.

Amy laughed. 'I know right?'

'Race you to the end,' said Emilia suddenly, and immediately she kicked away from the wall and shot through the water at speed. A moment later, a startled Amy took off after her, giving chase.

'Slow her down,' she shouted to Cassian as she powered through the water. She laughed as he dipped under the surface and then leapt out like a shark, tackling his wife and dragging her down.

Amy shot by, with a clear run to the end but her victory was snatched when someone's hand took ahold of her ankle and pulled her backwards.

She struggled, laughing as Emilia wrestled her in the water, splashing and fighting, holding each other back. Then the two of them slowed down and kissed, standing in the shallow end, a few feet from their watching and smiling husbands.

Amy's hands slid up Emilia's wet back as the blonde girl's tongue pressed between her lips, her fingers squeezing into the cheeks of her bottom as they moaned into each other.

They kissed and floated, pressing their bodies together tightly as their hands and fingers ran wild with a sudden and urgent passion. The men looked at one another and then moved closer, Mark sliding his hands around his wife as Cassian did the same to Emilia.

They both turned at their touch and swam into their arms, kissing them deeply, the two girls backs pressed together, their feet and toes touching and curling as they drifted along the bottom.

Emilia could feel Cassian's relief, his bulging shorts pressing into her crotch as they embraced, the warm water lapping around them as they bobbed and floated.

As her husbands arms slid down her back towards her bottom, Amy's hand intercepted it.

'Not so fast, cowboy.'

Cassian frowned, looking over his wife's shoulder as she turned her neck.

'I want to play a little game,' said Amy. She raised her eyebrows and then lowered her hands beneath the water line, sliding them down over her hips and hooking her fingers into her bikini bottoms. She tucked her legs up in the water and slipped them off, raising them out of the water on one finger.

'Em?' she said, nodding downwards at her crotch below the surface.

'You want me to take mine off too?' she said, shocked.

'Get 'em off,' said Amy, grinning.

Emilia stared and shook her head in disbelief as she looked from Amy to Mark and then Cassian. The two men shrugged.

She turned back and mock rolled her eyes, then somewhat reluctantly followed suit, undoing the string bow at her hip and sliding them off.

'Throw them to me,' said Amy. 'Mark, grab the two life rings.'

Mark frowned, pushing away and swimming over to the edge and then launching himself out of the pool in a torrent of water before unhooking each life ring and throwing them in.

Amy grabbed the first and tied Emilia's bottoms beneath it, hiding them as best as she could, and then she did the same with her own.

From the side, they were identical.

'Ok, turn around,' she said as Mark jumped back in. With them all facing away, she muddled them around to the stage where even she didn't know whose was whose.

Finally she swam them both to the far end of the pool and hooked them onto the side so they floated and stayed put against the wall, bobbing up and down gently.

'Ok. This is a three stage *boys race* to the finish. First stage, press ups. Fifty each.'

Mark laughed and looked at Cassian, who gave him his best, *bring it on* face.

'Second stage is running, three laps of the garden,' she nodded toward the patch of greenery adjacent to the pool.

'Stage three is swimming. Three lengths each, but,' she held up her hand and smiled. 'You have to swim through both of our legs underwater, once per length.'

Emilia's eyes grew wide and she covered her mouth and laughed.

'Winner, has their choice of life ring, and a chance to have your way with one of us. Right here. Right now. Runner up, gets the best consolation prize in the world.'

Emilia was now bright red and buzzing with excitement.

'Fuck yes,' said Cassian, swimming towards the side. 'Let's do this.'

Emilia watched as he climbed swiftly up and out onto the side, heading towards a wide flat area of grass. A moment later Mark joined him. She drifted over towards Amy and the two of them swam closer, laying their arms flat on the edge of the pool to watch.

Cassian knelt down first, followed a moment later by Mark, who looked over at him with a piercing gaze.

'Down we go,' said Amy. 'I'll count for Mark, and Em will count for Cass.'

The two men dropped to the floor, arms in the ready position, poised with their backs straight, biceps bulging as they prepared for the challenge.

'May the best man win,' said Mark.

'Oh, I will,' laughed Cassian, winking.

'Ready? Three, two, one. *Go.*'

Both of them dropped down simultaneously, noses touching the grass with each powerful dip.

'One, two, three,' shouted the girls in unison, yelling in their excitement.

Their strength was breathtaking and Emilia found it hard to concentrate, the idea that these two men were competing for their chance to make love to her and Amy was both primitive and utterly thrilling.

After another few lifts, Cassian was beginning to feel the strain and for a brief flash he glanced at Mark only to see absolute concentration on the man's face. He was powering on, with ease.

The count began to diverge, with Emilia slowing down and dropping behind Amy.

'Thirty one, thirty two,' she said, each one slightly slower than the last as Amy continued on relentlessly following Mark's steady pace.

As Amy approached the high forties, Cassian slowed right down and dropped to the floor with just eight to go as Mark leapt up to a cheer from his wife and began his first lap around the garden.

'*Come on Cass*,' said Emilia, laughing but rooting for him. 'Don't give up on me now.'

Her support spurred him on and he glanced at the pair of them, hanging onto the side of the pool, naked from their waists down and grinned.

He powered through the final seven and burst up with a renewed energy.

Running was his forte.

He tore after Mark, adrenaline bursting through him as he skidded into the first corner and immediately picked up his pace again.

Emilia began to cheer, almost jumping out of the pool as he began to catch up with Mark's steady, careful sprint.

As Cassian approached the second corner he skidded again but this time he lost his balance and slid down onto his side, losing valuable seconds as Mark tore on.

Back on his feet he scrambled forward into the second lap, struggling to maintain his grip and finally finding his pace again as Amy cheered Mark onward, jumping up and down in the water and proving to be quite a profound and beautiful distraction.

As the third lap commenced, Cassian was only a few feet behind Mark and the two girls shouted as he closed on him, now neck and neck as they headed towards the pool.

'Oh shit,' said Amy, grabbing Emilia's arm and turning to face her in panic. 'We need to be legs!'

Hurriedly as the two men dived in one after the other, the

two girls swam to the middle and then stood like starfish under the water, laughing in fear as their husbands powered towards them.

Mark reached Amy first, squeezing through her little legs and pushing her up out of the water as he shot through, heading straight for Emilia next who squealed as he neared her, not even pausing to come up for breath.

Amy managed to get back into position just as Cassian grabbed her lower leg and thrust himself through, spinning her around and sending her crashing under again.

Emilia screamed as the huge bulk of her husband threw her up and aside, splashing her down under the water and fighting to right herself before leaping back up and cheering them on.

She barely had any time to recover before Mark was on his way back, making a beeline for her bare legs again as Cassian tailed him only feet behind.

She braced herself as he slipped through, squealing as he shot beneath her, and then jumped slightly as Cassian glided under her, his shoulder accidentally teasing her naked lips.

She spun around to watch as Amy cowered before them, approaching almost level with one another, and then she burst into laughter, screaming as the three of them collided, dragging her under with them.

It was Mark who recovered first, bursting forward toward the far end as Amy exploded up and rubbed her eyes clear of the water.

'Split!' she shouted to Emilia. 'They're too close!'

Emilia swam to the right as Amy shot left and the two girls spread their legs again as the two men flipped underwater and powered back down the pool towards them.

They approached side by side. Neither of the girls were sure in all the excitement and chaos which was which. Both men squashed beneath them, low down as they almost hugged the floor of the pool and raced towards the finish.

The two girls spun to watch who would emerge first and they cheered as both men erupted from the water. But it was Mark who broke the surface in the right place, grabbing ahold of his life ring trophy and holding it aloft above his head as Cassian searched blindly for his own, finally turning and grabbing it before realising Mark had beaten him.

Cassian threw himself backwards in defeat, slipping under the surface of water as their wives cheered on, laughing in joy and clapping.

'Who did you win?' shouted Amy, glancing up at the ring he was still holding high in celebration. He looked up and unhooked the garment, then he winked at his wife and produced Emilia's white string bikini bottoms.

Emilia immediately blushed and her stomach filled with butterflies beneath the water as she saw her swimwear and her modesty being proudly held in the handsome, soaking wet, muscle bound man's arms.

Cassian resurfaced and looked across, bowing down to Mark as he grinned at his wife. After wiping his eyes clear he swam over to his friend, hand outstretched.

'Well played, mate. Well played.'

'Thanks pal. I think it's time to claim our prizes,' he laughed and nodded towards the women.

Emilia bit her lip as Cassian glanced towards Amy. 'You are the best consolation prize in the world,' he said as he began to swim towards her.

Mark watched for a moment and then set off towards Emilia, who was trying to stop herself from jumping out and running back inside. Cassian and her had made love on the side of a jacuzzi on their honeymoon, but she had never made love in a pool before. She'd never even been skinny dipping and the idea of it was suddenly incredibly intimidating, but she stayed put, grinning uncontrollably as Mark powered towards her. She reached out for him as he drew near and he scooped her up out of the water in both his arms, kissing her deeply as he swam her away.

A part of her was glad it was him and not Cassian. It was a part of her that she wasn't ready to confront or understand yet, but as Mark carried her to the edge of the pool she looked back towards her own husband and smiled.

As Cassian approached, Amy swam away in a backwards crawl and up to the edge of the pool, turning at the last moment, her feet unable to touch the bottom as he floated in behind her. She flashed a grin as she felt the tip of his cock brush against her backside through his shorts, the material drifting across the top of her thighs.

His feet could touch the bottom here and he planted himself firmly behind her as he wrapped his arms around her waist and leaned around to kiss her lips and neck.

'I've missed you,' he whispered.

'I've missed you too.'

His hands slipped further down and she felt his thumbs try to hook into the sides of her bikini bottoms, forgetting that they were still attached to the life ring floating around the pool. He laughed as he realised his mistake and she turned her head and raised her eyebrows at him, grinning.

A moment later she sensed him pulling down his swimshorts through the movement in the water. Then he floated closer, his cock pressing between her cheeks and sliding up and down against her forbidden hole, making her feel shameful with desire.

Then he pushed up and forward and slipped inside her pussy.

She moaned as she braced one hand against the wall of the pool and slid the other around the back of his neck, pulling him closer to her as he kissed her. His cock throbbed inside of her as he slipped in and out and she gasped as his fingers slid between her legs and began to circle her clit.

It felt different underwater, it was slower and Cassian seemed to be going deeper, pushing gently against her g-spot, as though he was exploring her with each long and smooth thrust.

It was heavenly.

She looked across at her husband and Emilia, smiling as she watched them kissing whilst trying to keep her eyes open as the slowly building, intense pleasure inside of her grew.

Mark swooped Emilia up, hoisting her bodily out of the water and making her bite her own lip in response to his strength. He carried her along a few metres and then placed her down so she was sat on a submerged seat at the shallow end, just a few inches below the water level.

From this vantage point she could see Amy, pushed hard up against the side of the pool, Cassian behind her, embracing her tightly as they fucked.

The surface here was at hip height for Mark and he wasted no time parting her legs, sliding himself up and pressing just the tip of his cock against her bare pussy, hidden beneath the now warm water.

Emilia reached between her thighs and took hold of him, sliding him back and forth, up and down across her clit and then back to her opening where he pushed gently into her, just a little way, his eyes working their way up and down her wet and glistening body.

A naughty thought crossed her mind and she stole a glance across at Cassian and Amy and grinned. As much as she wanted Mark inside her, she wanted Cassian to reclaim her first, and yet she knew she wasn't ready for that yet. Not yet.

As he pulled out of her again, Emilia slid him down further until he was pressed against her tight little rear entrance and then she smiled as his expression changed.

'Are you sure?' he said, his cock hardening as he spoke.

She nodded quickly, the now familiar taboo sensation spreading out from her chest and her legs. Without hesitating Mark braced himself and then pushed and to Emilia's surprise he slid in almost immediately, causing her to cry out involuntarily and throw her head back.

'Oh *fuck*.'

'Are you okay?' he froze.

'Uh-huh,' her body shook as she exhaled. 'Keep going.'

He did so, pushing slowly but firmly until he was fully inside her, then he waited again as she opened her eyes, a slow and soft moan escaping her lips.

She nodded for him to continue and he pulled out, just an inch, before thrusting himself back into her sweet forbidden hole as that incredible, unmistakeable feeling of fullness made her body tremble with illicit pleasure.

She tilted her head back, her eyes closed, leaning onto the palms of her hands as her girlfriend's husband's thick girth stretched her and made her feel whole.

She jumped as his thumb began to circle her and grinned at him as the two sensations hit her at once, then she reached down and took his hand, moving it lower, just above where his cock was sliding back and forth, and pressed him between her lips, inviting him inside her lips as her own fingers began to press urgently against her clit.

His large hand parted her and he curled himself inside her warmth, pressing up against her g-spot as his cock throbbed and strained in her ass.

Amy turned her head as Emilia moaned in pleasure and a moment later Cassian slipped out of her and spun her round, wrapping his arms around her waist and lifting her weightless body up as she wrapped her legs behind him. Then he swept her through the water until they were next to Emilia and Mark, sitting her down next to her girlfriend.

Emilia's eyes fluttered and she glanced sideways, leaning

slightly and reaching for Amy's face, finding her lips as Mark continued to make love to her.

Amy's hand slid down her chest, joining her fingers and sliding against her clit as Cassian took hold of her again and parted her thighs.

The water here was shallow and felt warmer than before as Cassian's cock glided back inside her, and a moment later she felt Emilia's fingers pressing against her sweet spot, their arms crossed as each other's husband fucked them harder and harder.

Mark was close. Emilia knew now what it felt like before he came and it instantly brought her to the edge.

It felt incredible.

Mark, inside her sweet forbidden canal, his fingers in her pussy curling against her g-spot as Amy circled her button. Cassian fucking her girlfriend, making her moan and throb and twitch and cry out.

She looked at her husband and found him smiling at her, his eyes beginning to roll into the back of his head as his muscles started to tighten and strain. Amy's fingers sped up and her arm straightened as she felt Cassian's cock throbbing and twisting as he prepared to fill her up.

'I love you,' she said to all of them, and then she looked at Mark and begged. '*Come inside me.*'

She cried out again as he grew within her and a moment later she shuddered and bent forward, looping her arms around his neck as they came together.

Even with the warmth of the pool water surrounding her she could feel his love pumping into her, his arms wrapped tightly around her as his knees gave way.

She looked sideways as she orgasmed, trying to keep her eyes open and smiling at the sight of her husband unloading into Amy, thrusting forward over and over as he buckled and came.

She loved seeing their faces, watching them pleasure each other. Seeing them kiss and embrace as they came down.

It was heaven.

It must have been that way last night, for him and for Alice.

It must have been beautiful.

Cassian lifted Amy's limp and satisfied body down into the water and Mark did the same, carrying the pair of them deeper into the pool.

As they neared each other, Amy reached out and clung to them and together they floated in the shallow water, holding each other. Their eyes closed, their arms wrapped tightly around each others wet bodies.

Together.

Blissfully happy.

*

Emilia lay on Cassian's chest, sprawled across the bed in their little room, her hair wet and her skin still damp as they dried off together in the afternoon heat.

She was still wearing her bikini top, and as they'd stepped back inside she'd wrapped the little sarong back around her waist, but her bottoms were still floating around in the pool, attached to the abandoned life ring.

She laughed quietly to herself at the thought and Cassian squeezed her into him as she did so.

'I love you,' she said, turning to look up at him.

'You are amazing,' he said, quietly and kissed her on the forehead.

After all making love together they had stepped out of the pool in the height of the mid afternoon sun and headed back into the villa for some shade and a little time to unwind with a brief siesta.

It was the first time they had been truly alone since Emilia had left to board a plane with Mark and Amy the day before.

Her head was filled with questions, and a big part of her was too afraid to ask them. She didn't want him to be dishonest, but she was afraid that by asking the things she felt compelled to know, he might feel the need to be untruthful, to avoid hurting her feelings. He was an honest man, she knew that, but perhaps it wasn't fair to put him in that position?

Still, she had to know. It was part of her coming to terms with it.

'How was it?'

Cassian looked down at her as he stroked her hair.

'How was what?'

'You know what I'm talking about.'

He hesitated, before nodding. 'Alice.'

She laughed and nodded too. 'Alice.'

'Do you really want to know?'

'She already gave me the highlights,' she said, as she doodled shapes on his chest.

'You spoke to her?'

'No, she texted.'

'What did she say?'

'Your ego is already *way* too big, no chance I'm telling you.'

Cassian laughed. 'It was nice,' he said, after a while.

'Nice?'

'It didn't feel wrong.'

She smiled and nodded.

'Did you cuddle?'

'Yes.'

'Was she happy?'

'Very.'

'And you did it twice?'

'Guess she mentioned that,' he raised his eyebrows.

'Emphatically, in capital letters in fact.'

Her husband laughed, shaking his head as he pressed his fingers into her skin, listening to her.

'The words she used were *His cock is like a magic fucking wand. I've never come that hard in my life.*'

Cassian erupted into laughter at this, bolting upright in bed.

'I knew I shouldn't have told you,' said Emilia, laying back on her pillow and covering her eyes with her hands.

'*Wow*,' said Cassian.

Emilia sat up and looked at him, her expression changing to a more serious one. She reached out for his hands and took them in hers.

'She said she'd like to do it again. Is that something you'd like too?'

He nodded, somewhat hesitantly. 'I love you,' he said.

She smiled warmly and then leaned forward and pushed him down onto the bed with one hand, kissing him hard on the lips.

'On *one condition*. You don't get to excuse yourself from making love to me, because you're too tired from fucking her.'

She straddled his stomach, her naked torso tantalising visible through the sheer material of her sarong as she placed her hands on his chest. He surged at her touch, lifting her up off the bed and making her smile.

She reached behind herself and took his member in her fingers laying him flat against his own stomach, then as he settled back down she shifted backwards, sliding her lips slowly over the length of his hard cock, teasing him.

His cock pinned down, she slowly moved backwards and forwards, her wet pussy sliding up and down, over and around him as he held her waist and closed his eyes.

'Where did you do it?'

'Over the dining room table.'

'Such a *bitch*,' laughed Emilia, recalling her instructions last night. 'Where else?'

'Our bed.'

'Did you bend her over?' she let the tip of his cock slip into her for a moment.

'Yeah.'

'Did you spank her?'

Cassian nodded and moaned.

'Did you fuck or make love?'

'Both.'

'Did you cum?'

'Yes.'

'Inside her?'

'Yes.'

Emilia grinned and shook her head. 'Naughty boy.'

Cassian watched as she slid her hands down between her thighs and began to touch herself, gyrating back and forth.

'I love you,' she said as she leaned back.

'I love you too.'

She moved against him.

'Do you love her?'

'In a way.'

'Good.'

Emilia breathed in and shook as her body tingled with illicit pleasure. She threw herself forward and kissed his lips. Then she reached between her legs, finding his cock and guiding him home.

His true home.

She moaned into his chest as he filled her up. She didn't care if Amy and Mark heard her. This wasn't about them, this was about her and Cassian.

Reconnecting.

Becoming whole again.

Brianna Skylark

Being one.

His hands gripped her thighs as he strained and shook, smiling as she looked down to see his wide eyes, desperate not to come too fast. Desperate not to disappoint her. But she didn't care.

It was as though all of her fears and all of her worries were fading away and becoming insignificant. Their love for each spread like a light, moving slowly but surely through a thick fog of darkness, dissipating it, parting it and pushing it back until there was nothing but bright sunshine and clarity and love.

He could never disappoint her.

She wanted him to be unable to hold back, to be bursting with desire for her and she could feel that he was.

She squeezed and thrust and bit her lip and caressed her own breast as his cock grew and then she felt herself rise up off the bed.

He groaned and their fingertips touched and their hands clasped together and he exploded and moaned out loud, his deep voice echoing into the villa.

Emilia closed her eyes, feeling each thrust and pulse as he spilled inside her.

He *loved* her.

He *wanted* her.

He always would.

Nothing else mattered.

*

CHAPTER FOUR

'Time to get up!' boomed Mark voice through the door of the bedroom. 'We've got a two hour drive this morning and we're leaving in thirty minutes, ready or not.'

Emilia's eyes shot open and she blinked and yawned, untangling her naked body from Cassian's.

'Oh shit,' she mumbled as she squinted at the clock on their side table. It was six thirty in the morning.

'Where are we going?' groaned Cassian, his eyes still half closed.

'I don't know,' she sat upright and rubbed her face. 'It's a surprise, I guess?'

'An *early* surprise.'

He reached out and pulled her backwards towards him, his large hands tight around her lithe waist. She giggled and screamed as he wrestled her, rolling into his arms as she fell onto the bed again.

'I don't think we have time,' she said, kissing him on the

lips.

'What I have planned won't take long.'

She laughed and pushed herself up and away. 'Come on, we need to get a shower.'

'Two birds one stone,' said Cassian swinging his legs off the side and standing up. He turned around to reveal his rock solid member.

Emilia covered her mouth, looking down at it, then back up into his eyes. She chewed her lip and felt herself shake with excitement.

'If you're really quick?'

Cassian nodded with enthusiasm.

She leapt up off the bed and grabbed his hand in hers, tugging him towards the ensuite shower as she laughed.

She turned on the tap and screamed as cold water shot out, leaping back as Cassian followed her in, pushing her up against the wall, her ass facing him.

He parted her legs as the water warmed up, rivulets running down both of their bodies as steam began to rise up from the floor. Then he pushed inside her hard, thrusting her forward.

Quickly he pounded into her, holding her hip with one hand as the other pinned her arms in place above her head. She angled her bottom backwards, so he could thrust more easily, moaning as his thick hard cock slid in and out of her.

It felt urgent and raw, and though she knew it wasn't true, it was as though he didn't care about her pleasure, just his own desire to fill her with his seed, to claim her again and again.

To make her *his*.

She felt him buckle and pulse and then he moaned deeply into her ear as he came, pressing his hard body against her as he kissed her over and over. Then he slipped out and smiled as he caught his breath.

She turned around, sensing the warmth of his love inside her as the shower continued to flow over them both, then she looped her arms under his and cocooned herself in him, relishing in the warmth and love of his body as he leaned into her.

After a few more moments, with Cassian regaining the strength in his legs, they stood up straight and looked at each other and smiled. They didn't need to say anything, they both knew.

Emilia was first out, wrapped in a thick soft towel, tucked into the little gap between her breasts, her hair wet but already drying in the warmth of the morning.

'What should we wear?' she called out to Cassian as he dried off in the steamy little room.

'I don't know, maybe ask Mark?'

'Mark?' she called out.

'You okay?' said Amy, from outside in the corridor. 'Can I come in?'

'Yes of course.'

Amy pushed open the door and stepped inside. She was wearing a similar bikini to yesterday, but she'd added a pair of high waisted shorts to the ensemble and a sheer lace shawl. On her head she wore a wide brimmed hat with a flower pattern bow tied around the top. She looked amazing and Emilia smiled as she walked in.

'That answers my question,' she laughed.

'What to wear?'

'Yep.'

'Mark wanted today to be a surprise but I don't think he understands quite how women think yet.'

'So, the beach?'

'Not telling you.'

'A little hint?'

'This,' she waved to her clothes. 'Is all the clues you're

going to get.'

Cassian stepped out of the shower room naked and walked confidently across the room. Emilia giggled as Amy's eyes looked straight down at his bare crotch.

'Morning,' she said, blushing a little. 'Nice time in the shower?'

'Great thanks,' said Cass as he pulled on a pair of boxers.

'So are we going rafting then?' he said, looking at her and laughing.

'How the *fuck?*' she said, confused at his apparent prescience.

'Wet bag,' he pointed at the rolled over waterproof sack that Amy had stashed in the corridor behind her before coming in. She turned around and sighed.

'You weren't meant to see that.'

'We can keep a secret.'

'Rafting?' said Emilia, a look of concern flashing across her face.

'Kayaking, but that's all I'm saying.'

'Don't worry,' said Cassian, looking over at his wife. 'You've been up and down the Cherwell plenty of times with Alice, it won't be much different than that.'

'Maybe a *little* different,' winked Amy raising her eyebrows as she turned around.

'You should call Alice today too,' he said as Amy left the room. He stepped into a pair of shorts and pulled them up and then reached for a thin button up shirt, doing up just the lower two thirds, before pocketing his phone. Emilia was still standing in her towel, her mouth open.

'Come on, Em. Let's go!'

'What? I'm not ready.'

'Hurry up then!'

'Are you kidding me? You wanted a quickie in the shower!'

'And now I'm dressed and ready to go.'

'You suck.'
'I love you too.'

*

The steps down to the gorge were uneven and sloped. They had been hewn into the rock face and gradually worn away by thousands of visitors over many years. At some point someone had hammered large metal pins into the side of the cliff and strung rope between them to create a safety banister of sorts and it was to this that Emilia clung as she made her way down towards the river.

Mark was a few paces in front of her, dressed in cream khaki shorts and a light blue button up shirt. Much to Emilia's frustration he seemed to take each step in his stride, turning occasionally to ensure that she was okay.

Amy was a few steps behind her, chatting animatedly with Cassian as she concentrated on not stumbling and falling to her death in the ravine below.

As they rounded the corner she was relieved to see that they had finally reached the canyon base and the beauty of the shallow river that carved through it.

All of the kayaks were painted flame red and ice blue with a fiery pattern extending along the length of each. It reminded Emilia of the line drawings she used to paint over as a child, of dragon's breathing fire onto old English castles.

The beach was shallow and thin and a wooden walkway extended along the shore with around ten boats, some single and some double, each one tied up to the wooden poles that jutted off the jetty.

A young, stunningly pretty instructor bounded along the pier towards them as they stepped off the last part of the track and pressed their feet into the milky sand. She was dressed in a tiny two piece red bikini that left very little to the imagination, surrounded by a sleek looking black life jacket which she'd half unzipped, making her breasts look like something out of a Jane Austen novel.

'Salut,' she said, brightly as she waved.

Emilia smiled at her enthusiasm and friendliness, waving back sweetly as the girl bounded and bounced up to them.

'Mon Dieu, vous êtes tous si *beaux*,' she said, admiring them all as they gathered.

'Je suis désolé je ne comprends pas, je suis anglais,' said Emilia with a sorrowful expression.

'She said, *you're all so beautiful*,' said Mark.

'Tu parles français?' said the girl, smiling at him in surprise and tilting her head to the side, her ponytail bouncing in the breeze.

'Oui j'ai étudié à Paris,' said Mark, smiling as the girl's eyes widened.

'Stop flirting, Mark, you've already got a wife *and* a girlfriend,' said Amy, popping up behind them and grinning at the young girl. 'Désolé, mon mari est un narcissique trop performant.'

Emilia didn't have to translate the word *narcissique* and grinned as the cute girl laughed and clapped her hands together, jumping up and down and then looking across at the boats before continuing. 'Ce n'est pas un problème, je m'appelle Celeste, es-tu excitée par ton aventure du matin?'

'Her name is Celeste,' translated Mark. 'And she's asking *if we're excited about our adventure this morning*.'

Emilia nodded enthusiastically and clapped, and then felt a little silly as Celeste looked at her with wide eyes and a huge grin.

'She's *so* cute,' said the little brunette in stuttered English. 'Ok, il y a quelques règles à suivre.'

'Down to business, here come the rules,' said Mark.

'Portez toujours votre gilet de sauvetage.'

'*Always wear your life jacket.*'

'Ne restez jamais debout dans votre kayak.'

'*Never stand up.*'

'Pas d'alcool.'

'*No alcohol.*'

'Et restez à l'écart des rochers en surplomb.'

'Erm, I think that was *stay away from the rocks above your head?*'

Celeste nodded and grinned, turning around and bending over for a little too long to collect two life jackets which she then passed to Emilia as Amy rolled her eyes.

Mark took one out of her hands and helped Emilia to put it on, zipping up the chest and tightening the side straps in place so it was secure. He then attached his own as Celeste checked Emilia's, nodding with satisfaction.

The little French girl then collected another set for Amy and Cassian, passing them over as Mark stepped down towards the shoreline and stretched. The sunshine hadn't yet reached into the gorge, but it was still warm down here in the shade. Amy couldn't help noticing the instructor stealing glances at her husband as he peered down river.

'Lorsque vous arriverez au bout, un autre instructeur vous guidera,' said Celeste as Amy and Cassian helped each other zip up.

Amy took over translation duties as Mark yawned. 'She said *when we get to the other end someone will help guide us in.*'

'Votre trajet devrait durer environ deux heures, allez lentement et profitez de la vue.'

'*It should take us around two hours and we should go slowly and enjoy the views.*'

'Merci beaucoup, Celeste,' said Emilia.

Mark turned around and delved into his pocket, then stepped toward the young girl, and handed her a fifty euro note with a wink.

'Oh mon Dieu, si généreux. Thank you, thank you so much.'

'Flirting again,' said Amy, shaking her head and walking towards him, she stood on tip toes and kissed him on the lips, her eyes admonishing him but her grin giving her amusement away.

Celeste laughed, a little embarrassed as she tucked the note into a waterproof pouch on her jacket. 'Ces deux sont vos kayaks,' she beckoned to them, pointing at a pair of red and blue two seaters nearest to where they stood. 'Qui va avec qui?'

'Who do you want to go with?' said Amy, turning to Emilia who shrugged.

Amy tilted her head to one side, thinking and then grabbed hold of Cassian's hand and tugged him toward the blue boat. Emilia giggled as Cassian followed, turning to join Mark as he held out his hand to help her into their red one.

'Oh, échange de femme,' said Celeste, raising her eyebrows as Amy sat down in her seat in front of Cassian, her bottom between his legs.

'Something like that,' said Amy as she leaned back, turning and kissing Emilia's husband before sitting back down and winking at the shocked Celeste who gasped, frozen in surprise. She looked to Mark to see his reaction and then laughed as he grinned back at her and shrugged.

'Polyamour?' she said, with wide eyes.

'Something like that,' said Amy again, smiling.

'Ooh la la,' said Celeste, fanning her face as she began to glow bright red.

Mark collected his oar, passing another to Emilia and then he started to slide the boat down into the water, pushing away from the shoreline.

Celeste called after them. 'Have a wonderful time, thank you so much. Please, come back soon.'

Mark waved and began to paddle as Emilia did her best to steer. She looked back to see Cassian and Amy coming up beside them, gliding along through the water and smiling.

'I think we made her day,' said Emilia as they came up beside.

'I think she'd quite like to join us for a night,' said Amy laughing.

'I wouldn't object,' interjected Mark, dryly.

Amy mock scowled at him and splashed him with her oar.

'Neither would I,' whispered Emilia quietly, turning her head to the other two men as they laughed.

Amy's mouth dropped open in shock.

'Are we not enough for you Mrs Emilia Black?'

'Ooh, you've been *full named*, she's angry now,' said Mark, guiding them gently around a bend in the gorge.

For a while they drifted along, paddling and chatting as the sun rose higher in the sky, enjoying the sights and sounds and the cool breeze as it swept along the water's surface from behind, like a smooth hand helping them along.

After a while the canyon opened up into a wide and shallow area, along one side of which was a beautiful waterfall that crashed down into the river from an overhang. It was stunning, like something seen only in nature documentaries.

Emilia stopped rowing, gently gliding along through the quiet waters as she looked up and around them.

Ahead the river narrowed around a wide and flat beach of stones, along the edge of which sat a handful of people, some dressed in swimming costumes, others sunbathing topless. Beyond them the rock face was sheer, extending up two hundred feet or more and topped with a lush canopy of greenery.

'Shall we explore?' said Mark.

Emilia nodded and together they began to row for the

shoreline, followed by Amy and Cassian. As they approached Mark powered forward, driving the kayak onto the stoney beach, then he stepped out and pushed until it was firmly lodged away from the waters edge. He stood up straight and offered Emilia his hand, helping her up and out of the little boat.

Cassian did the same, docking next to them and Mark offered his other hand to his wife, gently pulling her up and out until she was standing firmly on dry land.

The waterfall was sending a sheen of mist across the valley and the morning sun was creating a shimmering rainbow through it.

'Can we try and get a photo of all of us?' said Amy, reaching for her wet bag. She unclipped the waterproof sack and pulled out her phone as they all gathered round, then she flipped the camera to selfie mode as Emilia tucked in, the men standing behind the two girls and looking calmly into the camera.

'Smile,' she said as they all posed.

Satisfied, Amy palmed the phone, tucking it into the pocket of her life jacket and then turned to follow Mark as he made his way toward where the waterfall crashed into the river.

The mist was refreshing in the heat and Emilia understood why so many people were gathered here. With Amy and Mark ahead of them, and out of ear shot, she turned to Cassian, taking hold of his hand as she spoke.

'Have you heard from Alice?'

Cassian looked at her hesitantly and nodded.

'Is she okay?'

'She's good, I think she quite likes staying at ours.'

Emilia grinned. 'I bet she does. She's probably sleeping in one of your shirts.'

Cassian leaned down and kissed her. 'You should call her,

talk to her.'

Emilia nodded. 'I know, I will. It's just…'

'What?'

'Nothing. It doesn't matter. Is it okay if she stays with us?' she said as he pulled away. 'Until she gets something sorted?'

'Of course,' said Cassian, grinning and wiggling his eyebrows suggestively.

Emilia shook her head laughing. 'Not when I'm at home, okay? Do what you like with her when I'm out, but not when I'm at home. I'm sure you'd love to have us both at the same time, but that's not happening.'

'Disappointing,' he said as he pulled her closer to him, her eyes widening as she felt how hard he was through his shorts. Emilia slid her hand between the two of them and squeezed his girth with her fingers, kissing him hard on the lips.

'You'll have to wait until later I'm afraid. Maybe you should join Mark for a cold shower,' she said, nodding towards the muscle bound man, standing waist deep in the river beneath the torrent of water.

'I might have to,' said Cassian, looking down at the tent in his shorts. He rearranged himself and stepped back.

'Shall we go and join them?' she said.

'You should call her.'

'Why don't we paddle the kayaks over?' said Emilia, ignoring him. 'Go pick them up?'

'Ok,' he said. 'Let's do it,'

Hand in hand they made their way back to where they'd left the boats, pushing them slowly over into the water before climbing on board, drifting in the gentle current.

Emilia got control of hers and paddled over to where Mark and Amy were swimming, followed closely by Cassian. As they approached, Mark turned to watch, raising his hand up to shout.

'*Taxi.*'

Emilia laughed and steered her way over, deftly navigating the current generated by the falling water. Mark steadied her as she drifted close and swung the boat around, then he reached out for Cassian's oar, pulling both in tight either side of him.

Amy gracefully slipped up and onto the front of Cassian's, righting herself and then settling back down before Mark launched himself behind Emilia, balancing the boat again quickly and collecting his oar, before powering on.

Further up the river deepened and it became harder to see the bottom, either side becoming sheer cliff face. Emilia found it a little scary, and she tried a few times to touch the riverbed with her oar but was unable to do so, almost losing her balance in the process.

Although deep, it was still clear enough to see fish swimming beside them, some small and some large. Occasionally a big one would burst up from the darkness below and make a splash.

After another ten minutes the river widened again and Emilia began to relax, pulling alongside the others and smiling peacefully as they drifted along. As they rounded the next corner, the tall cliffs gave way to the buildings of a town through which the gorge carved.

They were tall and seemed to almost grow out of top of the sheer walls, merged by greenery and the occasional sprouting tree. Above them people sat on the walls and balconies, looking down hundreds of feet into the river below. Emilia waved at a sweet little girl in a flowery dress, excitedly pointing at them as they sailed by. As she waved back, Emilia felt an intense and almost overwhelming sensation in her chest that she immediately tried to subdue. Moments later the girl drifted out of sight and Emilia looked away and ahead, sighing.

She couldn't help it, she was starting to feel broody. She had been for a week or two now. She had tried to bury the feeling and there was a part of her that wondered if her behaviour over the last day had something to do with it all.

Right now though, she needed to focus on the present.

She wasn't sure how to reconcile the idea of having children with the complex situation she now found herself in, but as much as she tried to deflect away from it, her mind and her ovaries were heading in that direction.

'This is incredible,' she said as she drew level with Amy, reaching out for her hand. They pulled the boats closer until they butted together and held tight as they lay back in each other's husband's laps, drifting along in the warm sun and the cool breeze.

Above them a solitary bird circled in the sky, and the sun blazed down with a ferocious heat.

'Do you remember what you said to me in the sauna that day, the night before we first made love? You asked me - *What do we want?*' said Amy.

Emilia nodded, stroking Amy's thumb and said, '*For it to be nice.*'

'This is pretty nice isn't it?'

'It's better than nice,' she said. 'It's perfect.'

*

Emilia pushed open the door to the cafe and stepped inside. The decor was rustique, with thick brick walls to keep the heat out during the summer and to provide insulation during the winter. Large support beams adorned the ceiling, and towards the back the interior became more cave like. The serving area had been carved out of the rock, the chisel marks still visible. Emilia wondered idly how long the building had been here.

It was busy, and there were only a few places to sit but within moments an old, bearded man approached them, dressed in a traditional French waiters outfit, complete with waistcoat despite the heart, to direct them to the last few available seats.

'Suis-moi s'il te plait,' he said in a thick accent, beckoning them to come with him.

Mark waved the ladies forward and they followed along, as each of them weaved their way through the other diners to the rear of the establishment.

After lounging in the baking midday sun for a little too long, they'd continued on down the meandering gorge, eventually arriving at a little town that bordered the river. Overhanging buildings, built into and above the rock face hung down from them, precarious and foreboding, as though they might tumble down at any moment. There they were greeted by another jacket bearing instructor, male this time, who gestured them over and guided them in, helping them out one by one and tying off the boats to the little jetty.

He explained in broken English that they had a couple of hours in the town to grab some lunch and cool off before the minibus would be ready to return them back to the start and to have a wonderful afternoon.

Together they had wandered up through the cobblestone streets, climbing the steep steps together, Amy and Emilia side by side as Mark and Cassian followed, looking out for a nice restaurant where they could all eat.

As they sat down around the table, Mark ordered them a bottle of wine and a basket of bread and the old waiter scurried away to retrieve both, smiling happily to himself.

'My goodness,' said Emilia. 'That was amazing. I've never done anything like that before.'

Mark smiled and nodded. 'I'm glad you enjoyed the surprise. I've been wanting to do it for some time. Back when

I lived here, I travelled down to the Ardèche and spent a few days with a friend, paddling along the gorge there and camping beside the river. It's similar to this one, although perhaps in some places even more dramatic.'

'How does he have a story for almost everything?' laughed Cassian. 'I feel like I've barely lived and we're only a few years apart.'

Mark laughed. 'Stick with me mate and we'll find plenty of adventures to go on together.'

'I strongly suspect all of Mark's *friends* he talks about are his ex-lovers,' said Amy, raising her eyebrows at him accusingly. 'And he seems to have an awful lot.'

Emilia giggled and covered her mouth.

As Amy was about to continue talking she stopped and frowned as Mark's expression changed, a look of recognition crossing his face as he looked behind her, distracted by something.

She turned around in her seat to see the girl from the dock, standing at the bar ordering a drink, still dressed in her tiny red bikini but now wrapped in a black sarong which barely reached below her pert little bottom. Her hair was down now and even Amy had to admit to herself that the sweet little French girl was extremely pretty.

Mark grinned and looked at his wife, as she shook her head. Emilia looked between them, confused at the sudden pause in the conversation, frowning at Cassian who shrugged. She turned in her seat and looked around and then smiled shyly as she saw the girl at the bar. She too now turned and grinned at Amy who rolled her eyes at them both as Cassian finally caught on.

'Go on, invite her over,' she said, with mock reluctance.

'Celeste?' called Mark from the table, raising his hand.

'Of course, he remembers her name,' said Amy, rolling her eyes.

The girl turned, confused but with an expression of excited anticipation, looking toward their table. She grinned widely as she saw the four of them and Amy noticed that for a moment she actually bounced on the spot. She hurriedly turned back to the bar and paid for her drink and then she quickly made her way over to their table.

'Voulez-vous vous joindre à nous?' said Mark, smiling warmly and standing up.

'If that is okay?' she said, looking at Amy for permission more than the others.

'Please, we'd love you to join us,' she said, relenting at last.

Mark pulled up another chair from a nearby table as Emilia and Amy shuffled apart to give her some room between them as she excitedly sat down, smiling at them all.

'We can speak English,' she said, nodding. 'I like to practice.'

'Have you finished for the day?' asked Mark as he sat back down in his own chair.

'Yes, my shift is over,' she said in a subtle French accent. 'It's too hot for the boats to go out now, the Gorge goes to forty eight degrees some days at this time of year, it's too dangerous to work, so I break for the day and I have the afternoon off.'

'How long have you done this?' asked Amy.

'It's my third season,' she smiled and then shrugged. 'J'aime cela. It's the best job.'

'Where do you live?'

'In the city, I have a little apartment that overlooks the water gardens.'

'Sounds beautiful,' said Emilia, who was clearly taken with the girl.

'So… are you all together? Romantique?'

Amy smiled as Emilia blushed. Each of them looked at each other. They'd never considered themselves as being something which could be defined, but it was a question which had been hanging in all of their minds for some time. Now it was being asked and a mixture of reticence and anticipation murmured through the table.

'Yes we are,' said Mark, confidently as the others smiled.

'Et toi aussi?' she said, glancing between Mark and Cassian, who laughed.

'Non, juste les filles.'

'Ah, ok. So you échanger? Swap?'

'Oui,' said Mark grinning as he looked at his wife. 'Amy est ma femme,' he said 'My wife. And Emilia est la femme de Cassian.'

'And you share?'

Cassian nodded.

'That's so nice, tu es très chanceux. Lucky.'

Celeste turned and looked at both the girls with a shy expression.

'And do you two? How do you say?' she looked back at Mark. 'Faites l'amour?'

'Make love,' said Mark.

'Yes,' she turned back. 'Do you make love?'

'We do,' said Amy, taking Emilia's hand and squeezing it.

'That's so beautiful. Girls are better à brouter le minou than boys,' she giggled and turned a little red, pursing her lips.

Amy covered her mouth and laughed in shock as Emilia looked on confused.

'What does that mean?' she said, looking at Mark who shook his head, refusing to translate.

Amy leaned across Celeste and cupped a palm to her Emilia's and whispered. 'It's slang, but it means eating pussy.'

Her eyes grew wide and she went bright red, looking shyly at Celeste who was laughing quietly, covering her mouth in shame.

'How did you meet?' she asked, still giggling.

'It was at a masquerade ball,' said Cassian.

Celeste looked at Amy, puzzled.

'À un bal masqué,' she said, making her hands into the rough shape of a mask and covering her eyes.

'Ah oui,' she nodded. 'Excitant.'

'Do you have a boyfriend, or a girlfriend?' asked Emilia, trying to hide her red cheeks but failing.

'No,' said the girl, nonchalantly. 'I like to have fun though, with boys and girls.'

'Did you grow up here?'

'Yes, in the city with my mother,' she said looking down. 'She passed away two years ago now, so I live in her old apartment.'

'Je suis désolé pour votre perte,' said Mark, leaning forward and placing his hand on top of hers. Amy couldn't help noticing that Celeste stroked his thumb as he did so.

'What about you? Where in England are you from?' she said, brightly, trying to move away from the topic.

'We're from Oxford.'

'The Université?'

'Yes the same place,' said Cassian. As he spoke he felt his phone vibrate in his pocket and slipped it out, looking at the caller name.

It was Alice.

He frowned and glanced up at Emilia, but she was beaming at Celeste, her eyes wide and enchanted by the little brunette beauty, so he stood up and made his excuses, heading toward the front of the cafe, swiping to answer as he weaved his way out so it didn't go to voicemail before he had a chance to talk.

'Hey Alice,' he said as he stepped out onto the narrow cobbled street, walking over to a waist high wall which overlooked the gorge below.

'Hey,' she said. 'I wasn't sure you'd answer.'

'You okay?'

'I'm okay, I was just thinking about you.'

Cassian smiled. 'Were you thinking about my magic wand?'

'She told you then,' laughed Alice. 'I guess there's no secrets between the three of us anymore.'

'I guess not.'

'Is she okay?'

'She's great, more than great. It's beautiful out here. You should come with us some time.'

'You'd love that wouldn't you?'

Cassian laughed, turning around to face the cafe. Inside he could see Emilia laughing at something Celeste had said, touching the girls arm with her soft fingers.

'When are you guys back?'

'Saturday.'

'I miss you.'

'We miss you too.'

'We?'

'Alice,' said Cassian, warning her.

'I'm sorry, I know. It's just, the other night was amazing.'

'I know.'

'Did she say anything yet?'

Cassian hesitated, wanting to tell her how Emilia felt, but it didn't seem right coming from him. 'Yes, but it's best if you hear it from her.'

'Ok. I'm sorry.'

For a moment they both enjoyed a comfortable silence, Cassian smiling as he listened to her breathe. 'It was amazing,' he said finally.

'Can we do it again?'

He paused as he thought, turning back around and away from his wife. He looked out over the river. The beauty of the rocks and the trees and the blue flowing water down below was mesmerising. He watched, fixated as a bird dived down to the surface hundreds of feet below and plucked a small fish out using its beak, soaring back up high before disappearing into the thicket of foliage.

'Yes,' he said, finally.

Alice said nothing, but he could hear her relief, as though she was smiling down the phone.

'How's the house?' he said, changing the conversation.

'Good, but your cat is a nuisance.'

'We don't have a cat.'

Alice said nothing for a moment. 'Then the wild cat that has invaded your house is a nuisance.'

'So it's going well?' laughed Cassian.

'Peachy.'

'I love her,' said Cassian, suddenly.

'I know you do.'

'And I love you.'

'I know you do, and you can make me happy by repeating the other night once in a while. As long as it's okay with Em. That's all I want.'

'I want that too.'

For another few moments they listened to each breathing, until Cassian broke the quiet.

'I better leave you and the wild cat to it.'

'I miss you both,' said Alice.

Cassian turned back at last, looking in toward his wife. She had shifted even closer to the little French girl who was talking to her animatedly.

'We miss you too.'

'See ya, Mr Wizard.'

'See you, Alice.'

He felt guilty somehow. Despite Emilia's approval, something didn't feel right, but at the same time, it was what he wanted. But there was no way this could ever move forward without her.

He loved her more than anything. More than life itself.

He had to know she meant what she was saying, but he wasn't sure how to go about getting that kind of reassurance. Perhaps he just had to take her word for it?

He crossed the street, dodging a fast moving moped, then ducked back into the cafe, his phone still held tight in his palm.

As he made his way back to the table, Emilia turned to look at him and smiled broadly, beckoning him over with excitement in her eyes.

'Celeste has invited us out tonight,' she said, bouncing in her chair.

The young French girl turned in her seat, looking up at him with wide eyes.

'On peut aller danser. Dancing? Mark already paid for our drinks,' she said laughing in his direction and shrugging.

'Just the two of you?' said Cassian.

Amy looked at Emilia and Celeste who both smiled enthusiastically and nodded. 'We'd like that.'

'Ok, let's do it,' said Amy as she raised her eyebrows at Mark.

'Fine by me. Is that okay with you, Cass?'

'Of course, you and I can have a few beers back at the villa.'

'Should we meet you somewhere?' said Amy, turning to Celeste.

'It's a place called *Badaboom*,' she said, standing up to leave. 'At ten?'

'We'll be there.'

'I'm *so* excited, à bientôt.'

She leaned forward and kissed Emilia three times on her cheeks and then did the same to Amy. Then she turned and winked at Mark, holding up the fifty euro note he gave her earlier and flexing it.

'Maybe after the dancing, I can see you again? And your friend?' she raised her eyebrows, then turned around, walking away and swaying her hips as they all watched, open mouthed.

'Ok,' said Amy, grinning at Mark once their new friend was out of ear shot. 'Maybe you were right.'

He laughed and winked at her.

'She's lovely,' said Emilia, watching as the girl left, bouncing out into the street.

She was more than lovely, thought Emilia to herself.

Just like Amy, she was something special.

Cassian glanced down at his phone again, then slipped it back into his pocket.

*

As the taxi drew to a halt outside the club, Emilia peered out of the window excitedly looking for Celeste whilst Amy slipped the driver his fare.

The queue stretched beyond the corner, as they both stepped out onto the curb. The end was out of sight, wrapping around the side of the old building and disappearing into a side alley.

Amy had chosen to wear a loose beach dress which flowed smoothly around her thighs as she walked, with a lace back which drew together like a corset.

Emilia on the other hand had chosen a little red dress with a cross over strap that wrapped up from her waist and around her neck in a loose bundle of material, revealing a little round circle of under cleavage which she was feeling rather self conscious about.

Amy looked up and down the breadth of the mass of

people and then spied their new friend's now familiar face waving back at them from near to the front, beckoning to them both to come and join her.

Emilia frowned as Amy reached out. 'I can see her, let's go.'

'Shouldn't we join the back of queue?'

'I think it's okay,' she laughed. 'Come on.'

Emilia looked at Celeste as Amy dragged her forward and saw that she was shaking her head, giggling at her reticence. As they approached she opened her arms wide to embrace them. 'You English, you love queueing. It's so cute.'

She gently reached out and touched her waist, then kissed Emilia three times on her cheeks, deepening her blush with each peck, and a moment later she extended the same courtesy to Amy.

As she stepped back, Emilia couldn't help looking her up and down. She was wearing a stunning little zip up black dress with a lattice chest and spaghetti straps, revealing a tantalising glimpse of her ample cleavage, the sight of which made her heart thump a little faster in her already anxious chest.

'Have you been here long?' asked Amy over the noise of the crowd

She shrugged. 'Un quart d'heure?'

'Is this your favourite discothèque?' said Emilia, looking up at the baroque exterior as she tried to calm herself down. She hadn't been clubbing in almost five years and the mass of people were making her nervous.

'This place is *le meilleur*, you'll see,' she winked as the crowd began to move forward.

Inside, the venue was a heaving mass of sweat and flesh. Emilia could feel the bass in her chest as she followed Amy and Celeste through the throng of young people.

The music was ear splitting. Her chest pounded with each thump of the bass line as she felt it vibrating up through the floor. At the far end stood six, ten-foot tall speakers, behind and above which was a rig of scaffolding that extended high into the rafters of what appeared to have once been a magnificent auditorium or theatre. The original Art Deco furnishings were still visible, juxtaposed now with modern and minimalist modifications to the original facade.

Dry ice drifted in a layer around her knees as sprays of mist from jets situated on joists throughout the dance floor doused the assembled revellers, keeping them cool in the deep heat of the Mediterranean summer.

As the crowd thickened she reached out and took hold of Amy's hand, the touch of her skin making her heart pound louder than the beat as they slid their fingers together. She was often too self conscious to hold Amy's hand in public, but somehow it seemed okay whilst they were hidden amongst the hundreds of revellers. Slowly they made their way through the crowd, pushing and jostling as they edged towards the bar, led by the graceful hips of their new friend Celeste.

Emilia watched in awe as she forged her way through to the front, twisting around and beneath people almost twice her size and stature without so much as raising an eyebrow through a deft mixture of guile and charm.

'What would you like to drink?' she shouted over the noise.

'Strawberry Daiquiri?' said Emilia.

'Mojito?' said Amy.

'Cuban, nice,' Celeste nodded her approval and Emilia flushed in relief, a brief excited smile crossing her lips as the French girl grinned at them both. 'I think I'll join you and have a Mojito too.'

She turned around and waved, immediately catching the eye of a tall, sweaty and incredibly gorgeous bartender who leaned across the counter, placing his face flirtatiously close to hers. She spoke into his ear, slowly and carefully, grinning as he turned to face her, then he winked and threw himself backwards, swinging into action.

'What did you say to him?' said Amy, placing her hand in the small of Celeste's exposed back.

'What he wanted to hear,' she replied, grinning.

A moment later there was a flurry of movement and the man slid one tall red cocktail and two small blue one's across the bar. As Amy waved the money at him, he grinned and winked, glancing from Celeste to Emilia and making her blush as his eyes met hers, then he turned away to the next customer without so much as another glance.

'Doit être gratuit?' she said, collecting all three drinks and passing them back to the girls.

Amy led the way back out, moving away from the bar and toward a seating area with tall seats and tall tables. They found one a little way from the dance floor, loud enough to enjoy the music but quiet enough to hear their own voices.

'So how long have you lived in the city, Celeste?'

'I was born here, in fact my mother gave birth to me in the apartment I live in now,' she laughed as she sipped her drink.

'Really? Gosh,' said Emilia.

'So, I've lived here all my life,' she shrugged. 'I love it.'

'It's such a beautiful city,' smiled Amy.

'Now come on,' said Celeste, leaning forward excitedly. 'How does it work with you guys? Do you live together? Are you in love?'

Emilia blushed again and glanced at Amy who laughed.

'We don't live together, no. We met just over two months ago.'

'Two months?' she said in shock. 'It seems like you've known each other *forever*.'

Amy smiled and nodded. 'It feels like that to me too.'

'So you're in love then?'

Emilia laughed and looked away.

'Have you told each other?' she asked, grinning back and forth between them.

Emilia nodded and bit her lip, looking across at Amy and blushing.

'You have!' laughed Celeste. 'You guys are so *adorable.*'

'We have,' conceded Amy, smiling at her.

'Is the sex *really* hot?' she whispered, laughing. 'I bet it is.'

'*So* fucking hot,' laughed Amy, as Emilia squirmed. 'Em is *really* dirty.'

'Is she?' laughed Celeste, turning to face her as she tried to sink into her seat. 'I thought she would be, the innocent ones are always the dirtiest, you know?'

'The first time we had sex,' said Amy, getting closer to Celeste as Emilia's eyes widened. 'She took both our husbands at the same time, one in her pussy, the other in her *ass.*'

Celeste's eyes grew wide as she turned back to Emilia.

'Is that so?'

'I hate you,' said Emilia, smirking as her face glowed.

'It's *true*, wow! I've never done that before,' she leaned forward. 'What was it like?'

'Oh my goodness,' said Emilia, hiding her face and laughing. 'Can't we talk about something else?'

Celeste laughed and turned back to Amy. 'I think we've broken her.'

'I think we have,' she smiled, trying to catch her eye behind her fingers before relenting. 'Maybe we should talk about something else.'

Emilia nodded and slowly reappeared, smoothing the edges of her skirt and adjusting herself before making eye contact with Celeste who burst into laughter again.

'I hate you both.'

'Je suis désolé,' she said, bowing her head.

'Me too,' said Amy, winking. 'So come one, change of topic, why don't you tell us about the book you're reading Em?'

Emilia blushed again and glared back at her girlfriend, scowling at her. 'Do you really want to know? Or do you just want to be mean and make me feel awkward again?'

'I really want to know,' she said, propping herself forward on her elbows. 'Honestly, I do.'

Emilia looked at her, glaring into her eyes, probing her, before giving in and then smiling faintly. 'I'll tell you a bit about the *first* one,' she said, trying to hold back her obvious passion. 'But not the second. It would spoil too much and I really want you to read it.'

'Go on,' said Amy, as she smiled at Emilia's excitement.

'What book is this?' said Celeste, looking confused and turning her head back and forth between them.

'*The Paramour*,' said Amy. 'It's a naughty book series.'

'Naughty?'

'*Full* of sex,' laughed Amy.

'Oh, nice,' she giggled and turned to Emilia, who was squirming in her seat.

'Ok. So, the husband of Lady Victoria Rosewood is *murdered* by someone, but we don't know who. Her sister-in-law, who happens to be the Duchess of Kilburn-'.

'Of course,' laughed her girlfriend.

'*Of course*,' she nodded, grinning. 'Well she, and her notorious and intimidating husband the Duke, invite her to stay with them in the highlands of Scotland for a few weeks to allow her time to grieve away from the London press, whilst also offering to help her investigate her late husband's murder.'

'Intriguing,' said Amy. 'So when do they all start shagging?'

Emilia laughed and blushed. 'It doesn't take long,' she said, screwing up her face. 'But it's nice though, it's kind. It's not porn.'

'*It's not porn*,' laughed Amy. 'What a recommendation.'

'Is this *La Maîtresse*?' said Celeste, suddenly.

'Maybe?' said Emilia, looking across at her. She found it hard to keep her eyes from glancing down at the open lattice top and the barely concealed curves of the girl's ample chest.

'It sounds *le même*, the same,' she nodded.

'Have you read it?'

'Many times,' she laughed. 'It's *very* naughty. What else do you both like to read?'

Amy looked away, thinking, then she turned back with a cheeky smile on her face. 'I really like horror.'

'Horror? Why?' said Emilia.

'I like being scared.'

'Is that why I'm still having nightmares about our first date?'

'I'm not sure that was our first date,' laughed Amy.

'Whatever it was, every time I look out of a darkened window I half expect *Annie*, the animatronic porcelain doll to be staring back at me, her eye sockets melting in flames.'

'What happened on your first date?' said Celeste, looking concerned.

'Amy took us to an, erm… escape room?'

'Where you have to do the puzzles?'

'That's it, but this one was haunted by the ghost of a little girl and her creepy possessed doll, Annie. I performed my first exorcism that night and I was *not* expecting that.'

Amy was now laughing so hard she was almost crying.

'I'm so sorry,' she said, wiping tears away from her eyes.

'So what makes you like being scared?' said Celeste, turning to face her.

'I don't know,' she waved her hands across her face, trying to calm herself down. 'It's kind of sexy though isn't it? The feeling of being scared? It's arousing.'

'Yes, I get that,' said Celeste, grinning and nodding.

'No,' said Emilia. 'It is not.'

'It is,' insisted Amy. 'Not *actual* fear, but the *idea* of fear. Safe fear. Have you ever been to one of those Halloween Haunt events? With the actors and the sets?'

'No,' said Emilia, emphatically.

'It's amazing, you should come with us this year.'

'Oh good grief, *no* chance. I would actually pee myself.'

Amy laughed again, covering her mouth in embarrassment as Celeste laughed too. 'Yeah, I did that two years ago.'

'Seriously?'

'Just a little bit,' said Amy, holding up her fingers an inch apart.

'You're not convincing me.'

'In that kind of scenario though, it's scary, *really* scary, but you're not actually in danger. Not *real* danger. But afterwards? Oh my goodness, I get so horny.'

Emilia grinned as Celeste nodded knowingly.

'Last year?' she continued. 'We fucked in the back of the car.'

'I'm a little more intrigued.'

The music changed tempo and seemed to rise in volume as a recognisable tune began to play. A huge cheer from the crowd rumbled through the arena and various groups of party goers began to make their way to the dance floor.

Amy took a big swig of her Mojito as she giggled. 'So, did you manage to talk to Cass?'

'Cass is *your* husband, right?' said Celeste turning back to Emilia.

She nodded, and grinned, looking down into her drink and swirling the liquid around with the little cocktail umbrella.

'I take it you *reconnected* too then?' laughed Amy, before turning to Celeste with a wink. 'Baiser.'

Emilia's grin widened as the French girl nodded

knowingly.

'We did. Twice.'

Amy put her hand up for a high five. 'The man's a machine. That's *three* girls, *five* times, in just over twenty-four hours?'

She shrugged, the daiquiri beginning to go to her head. 'Fresh pussy.'

'*Emilia*,' Amy's face was a picture of shock.

'One drink and I'm little *Miss Potty Mouth*.'

'Wait, *three girls*?' interrupted Celeste, suddenly very excited. 'Who else is a part of your little ménage? Do you play with others too?'

Emilia looked down again, embarrassed and after a moment, Amy took over. 'Cassian slept with Emilia's *sœur* last night.'

'Your sister?' she said, a look of shock on her face.

She nodded and then shrugged, struggling to find the right words, then she laughed. 'In his defence. She's *really* fucking hot. I'd fuck her, you know… if she wasn't my sister… and if had a cock.'

'You're okay with this?'

'I think so, it's just sex,' she shrugged.

Celeste nodded for a while, as though she was processing this turn of events. 'You ever been fucked with a strap on?' she said suddenly.

Emilia blushed and burst into laughter at the tangent, shaking her head. 'No, I haven't. But we should try that,' she said glancing at Amy who grinned and then surprisingly blushed, looking away.

'It's strange,' continued Celeste. 'It's not like an *actual* cock, you don't feel like you're being fucked by a man. It's not a, um, a *remplacer*? Replace?'

'Substitute?' said Amy, feeling more than a little turned on now.

'Merci. It's not like that. It's just firmer, and stronger. And wearing it is fun too, you feel *puissante*. Powerful.'

'Maybe you could demonstrate it to us?' said Emilia, looking at Celeste for a little too long.

'Good grief, Em,' said Amy, interrupting their gaze. 'One drink and you become a sex fiend. What happens if you have two?'

'I don't know I've never had two in the same night,' she laughed, raising her eyebrows and taking another sip.

'More drinks please waiter!' shouted Amy to no one in particular. 'Seriously though, how does Cass have the stamina? I don't think Mark could manage that.'

Emilia shrugged as she took another swig. 'He hasn't met my sister… yet.'

'Oh my *goodness*,' Amy shook her head as she giggled and swigged a final gulp of her Mojito.

'Another drink?' Celeste reached for her empty glass and then looked to Emilia who grinned and swallowed the rest of hers.

'Are you trying to to get us drunk, Celeste?' she said, dabbing at her lips.

'Yes, I am,' she winked and plucked the glass from the table before jumping down from the little stool and wiggling her hips as she began to walk away. Both Emilia and Amy watched her as she disappeared into the crowd, before turning back to one another and grinning.

'She's so hot,' said Emilia, grinning and biting her lip before reaching out for Amy's hand, then hesitating and pulling it back. 'Do you think-'

'Yes, definitely,' said Amy, interrupting.

Emilia nodded as her grin exploded into a blushing smile.

'Do you think she wants to?'

'I have no idea, but I am so up for finding out.'

Emilia laughed as Amy reached out for her hand, gesturing

for them, but Emilia kept them in her lap.

'I love you,' she said.

'I know.'

Amy frowned and pulled her hands away, then twisted in her seat to look for Celeste at the bar. Unable to see her, she turned back. 'What's wrong?'

'Nothing.'

'Bullshit, you can't stop touching me when we're alone but you hesitate to take my hands now?'

Emilia looked down, ashamed. 'I just feel nervous about being *out* in public.'

'Why?'

'I don't know, I just don't want people judging us.'

'What does that even mean?'

'*I don't know*, people looking at us and thinking badly?'

'Does it matter? What do they know? They don't know us, they can't make that judgement.'

'I guess not.'

'Do you think Celeste cares?'

Emilia shook her head. 'I'm sorry.'

'I'm not offended, I just don't want you feeling ashamed. You've got nothing to be ashamed of.'

Emilia looked up at her and nodded, taking a deep breath. 'Thank you.'

Amy smiled and reached out for her hands again, making Emilia smile. She reached out for them and took them, but she couldn't help glancing around her.

'On another serious note,' said Amy, flicking her eyebrows. 'You and Cass *reconnected*, and you've talked, but is everything okay? I know you've rationalised all this, but if you're just burying it all away somewhere then that's not healthy. Have you spoken to Alice yet?'

Emilia blinked at Amy, and as she went to answer she faltered and stopped, looking down at the table and frowning before answering properly. 'I've been back and forth in my head about this all week and I've come to three conclusions,' she held up three digits dramatically in front of her. 'And they are... *drumroll please.*'

Amy laughed and began to drum her fingers on the table.

'I love Cass. He's my rock. He might get worn away over time, but he's dependable and solid and unmovable. Even if I wanted to, I don't think I could get rid of him.'

Amy nodded. 'Solid reasoning. So does that make me your *rack*?' she squished her breasts together and then continued the drumroll. 'Ba-dum-*tish*!'

Emilia shook her head, giggling at her girlfriend's awful joke before continuing.

'*And* I love Alice. She's the greatest gift my parents ever gave me and every day, all I want to do is live up to that ideal for her.'

Amy nodded, and stopped drumming as Emilia's eyes now fixed on her.

'And I love *you*. It turns out the man of my dreams is a girl. My Prince Charming is a princess. I want to be yours as much as I want you to be mine,' she reached out and took hold of Amy's hands again, confidently this time, squeezing them into her own. 'You make me so ridiculously, deliriously happy and all I want to do when I'm not around you is be around you, and when I am around you all I want to do is *really, really* rude things with you.'

Amy burst into laughter, drawing the attention of a nearby group of men and women. She glanced at them as they returned to their conversation and then looked back at Emilia, smiling.

'Have you called Alice yet?'

Emilia shook her head and Amy frowned as she flushed white.

'Still not ready?'

Emilia let go of her hands as she saw Celeste returning with another round of drinks.

'I had to pay for *these* ones,' she laughed and shrugged. 'Different boy. What did I miss?'

Amy glanced at Emilia and grinned, and then laughed as her girlfriend shook her head in panic, blushing. She turned her head on her side then raised her eyebrows and opened her mouth to speak, but then to her surprise, Emilia interrupted her.

'I was just telling Amy, about how much I want to kiss you.'

Amy's mouth fell open as Emilia smiled coyly and sipped her new drink.

Celeste smiled at her and laughed, not breaking eye contact. She slowly ran the tip of her tongue along the edge of her lip, before biting it and nodding. Then she turned to Amy.

'And what about you? Do you want to kiss me too?'

Amy froze. This wasn't how it usually went. *She* was normally in charge. She was the bold one, the cheeky one, the *rude* one. This wasn't normal.

She liked it.

'Maybe,' she said.

'Maybe? Or *fuck yes*?'

Amy jumped as she felt Celeste's fingers sliding up her inner thigh. Her knickers were already wet from all the flirting, but now they were soaked.

'Come on,' she said suddenly. She grabbed her drink and knocked it back. 'Let's dance.'

She stood up grinning and beckoned to Celeste and Emilia, reaching forward to take their hands as they both nodded and hurriedly finished their glasses. Together they weaved their way back through the tables towards the dance floor via a short set of illuminated stairs.

Emilia had assumed they would find a little spot near the

edge but it seemed Amy had other ideas, dragging them into the centre of the heaving mass of bodies, stopping suddenly and turning around.

Emilia fell into her, and the three of them laughed as they steadied each other, jostled by the hundreds of other dancers all around them. For several songs they all danced and jumped, gyrated and pounded their feet along to the music, laughing and smiling with others as they twisted and turned, but as they continued the room seemed to get smaller and smaller, and more intimate and private. Each of them stealing naughty glances at each other, tantalising glimpses of smooth skin and supple curves.

Emilia's whole body tingled as Celeste's hands touched her hips and she closed her eyes as their new friends smooth thigh slid between her legs and pressed against her as she moved to the music. Amy slipped her hands around Emilia's waist from behind and she in turn draped hers over Celeste's shoulders as each of them slowed down, swaying to the tune. They shuffled closer, grinding gently into one another.

It was something they weren't consciously trying to achieve, but gradually a small circle opened up around the three of them, a circle that no-one else seemed able to enter and somehow it felt completely natural.

Sweating, caressing, touching.

Skin on skin.

Hips on hips.

As they got closer and more intimate, the music seemed to fade away and become background noise. It was as though the shades were coming down on the world, fading everything out until it was just the three of them, pressing their bodies together with passion and urgency.

Emilia paled as she looked into Celeste's eyes, stealing a glance down at her glistening lips. Then she felt herself going weak at the knees as Amy kissed her neck, smiling and closing her eyes as Celeste's fingers tucked her hair behind her ear.

Then their lips met and her eyes filled with sparkles.

As she pulled away she turned her head and found Amy, kissing her deep and then she jumped and writhed as she felt someone's warm fingers sliding up her skirt.

She moaned and then she heard Amy gasp.

'Let's get out of here,' breathed Celeste in her ear. *'Now.'*

*

As the taxi drew away, Amy pushed Celeste up against the door of the villa, kissing her lips and sliding her hand through the lattice slits of her dress, squeezing her breast as Emilia fumbled with the keys, dropping them on the ground and swearing. Together the three of them bent down and swept their hands across the gravel looking for them and laughing.

Finding them, Celeste handed them back to Emilia who stood up and held them firmly between her fingers, doing her best to see the reflection of the lock in the moonlight as Amy kissed her neck. She scratched against the metal as Celeste's hand danced up her thigh, slipped beneath her dress and clenched around her bottom, squeezing her fingers inside the hem of her underwear.

As the door swung open, Emilia turned and wrapped her arms around the little French girl's neck, pulling her backwards and into the dark little corridor, running her index finger over her lips as they tried to stay as quiet as they could.

Stumbling and almost falling several times they made their way through to the lounge, stifling their laughter and doing their best not to giggle.

Emilia fell onto the couch and Celeste straddled her, reaching out and pulling her closer for another kiss as she slid her hand between her thighs.

'Je te veux en *moi*,' she said, pushing Emilia's fingers against her already soaking wet knickers.

Celeste reached behind Emilia's neck and pulled the loop of her red dress forward over her head and down over her shoulders as Amy's hands ran up her now bare stomach and over the lace edge of her bra, making her arch her back involuntarily and moan out loud.

Someone shushed her and she opened her eyes to watch as ever so slowly Amy slid one arm up Celeste's back and unzipped her dress, letting it fall down around her exposing her beautiful, pert and round breasts in the slivers of soft moonlight that filtered through from the garden.

Emilia's hands smoothed up the girl's toned abdomen and stroked her tight curves and then she laughed as she fell forward and began to kiss her lips and cheeks and neck with such enthusiasm that it made her squeal.

As Amy watched, stroking her fingers slowly down the brunette beauties back, Celeste began to kiss her way down Emilia's chest, pausing to undo her bra and then sliding it away and dropping it onto the floor, discarding it hastily. Steadily she kissed her way around her curves and then clamped her lips over her nipple as she squirmed and wriggled and cried out.

'I *love* how sensitive you are,' she said, looking up in surprise.

'She can't take it for long,' whispered Amy, giggling as her chest pounded.

Emilia grabbed the back of Celeste's head and pushed her down, moaning loudly as she carried on sweeping her tongue around her breast.

As Emilia writhed, Amy started to peck her way down the French girl's back, kissing the curve of her bottom, pushing her crumpled dress away to reveal more of her skin and making her arch up in anticipation.

Torturously slowly, Celeste kissed a line around Emilia's waist. Amy shuffled down as she pulled Emilia's dress down to her ankles, leaving her in just her cute lace knickers on the sofa. Then Celeste stood up and let her loose, unzipped little black dress fall completely to the floor. Slowly she crawled up and lay between Emilia's legs and pushed her underwear aside.

Emilia gasped as her fingertips slid up and down her parting, spreading her wetness up and down. Then a moment later, she cried out in pleasure as she felt her tongue pressing against her lips.

Her whole body felt alive with desire and lust as her new friend licked her. As she lay there, with waves of pleasure building up inside of her, she looked past at Amy grinning wildly as their eyes met. She ran her fingers through Celeste's hair and let out another gasping moan, struggling to stay quiet.

Then Celeste shifted to the side and she felt Amy come closer. As she looked down to see what was happening she felt her heart thumping hard in her chest. Amy knelt before her now too, looking beautiful and full of passion. Quickly her little redhead took hold of the hem of her own dress, pulling it up and over her head to reveal that she was wearing nothing underneath. Both of her girls were now laying on their front between her legs, which were spread wide open on the coach as they looked up at her, grinning mischievously.

They were both going to kiss her, *at the same time.*

She watched with her eyes wide as together, they lowered their heads toward her parting… and then she cried out, abandoning any pretence of remaining quiet as she felt both of their sweet tongues sliding across her warmth.

Fingers pushed inside her as lips kissed her clit and she

reached out both of her hands touching each of their cheeks as they pleasured her. Amy's tongue lapped against her clit as Celeste's ran up and down her parting. Then she felt them kissing each other and she looked down at their wet lips, glistening in the silvery light.

Then they turned back to her and kept going. She ran her fingers through their hair as they swept and swirled and she moaned as she started to feel that familiar sensation. That wave, that glorious wave, starting out now, building up far away in the ocean.

Everything felt different without the men. It didn't feel as urgent or as raw, it didn't feel like they were under pressure. Their expectations were different. This was gentler, kinder, softer.

Sweeter.

There was no rush, just playful enjoyment, and heavenly pleasure.

She reached down and found Amy's hand and squeezed it as Celeste's tongue rolled across her lips. It was as though she was tasting her, savouring the sweetness of her pussy. It felt beautiful and intimate and *oh so incredibly good*.

She sensed her look up.

'Ça fait du bien?'

Emilia nodded her head urgently, understanding, then she arched her back as another wave crashed through her, each one bigger than the last. Each swirl of her tongue more powerful and more urgent than the one before.

Amy's hand squeezed her own and then a moment later she heard and felt Celeste moan into her, as the little French girls fingers parted her lips, sighing softly as they slipped inside and arched upwards, curling and pressing smoothly against her sweet spot.

'Faster?' asked Celeste as Emilia nodded.

'*Yes.*'

She couldn't take much more, she reached down and gently cradled Amy's head as she started to orgasm, squeezing her thighs together and crunching forward as her body began to twitch and shake, her toes curling as they pressed against the edge of the sofa.

Then as she came, something new happened, Celeste arched her fingers tighter inside of her and pressed deeper and Emilia felt this sudden and powerful sensation, like pressure building up from within, but with nowhere to go.

She tried to stop it, tried to squish her thighs together in embarrassment, but Celeste held her firm and kept thrusting and curling as an intense warmth spread around her thighs and her tummy, intensifying with every passing second.

She gripped onto the sofa and flailed her arms, letting go of Amy as her eyes rolled backwards and her mouth opened wide.

She couldn't stop it, whatever it was - it wasn't going away, so she stopped fighting it, and relaxed.

Her face flushed.

She surrendered.

Relief.

She felt a gushing sensation between her legs as her whole body succumbed and melted, and in the distance she heard Amy gasp quietly.

She heard words, but they were far, far away and she was too relaxed to open her eyes.

Too peaceful.

A familiar hand slipped down her arm and into her palm, slender and delicate fingers squeezing her.

Lips on her own, sweet tasting and gentle.

Amy's lips.

'Did I pee myself?' whispered Emilia as quietly as she could, her eyes closed as she tried not to laugh.

Amy giggled. 'Sort of.'

As her senses returned she experienced a strange sensation, as though she was coming out of a deep and shameful sleep. Her eyes were hard to open but the more she tried the easier it became.

Amy and Celeste were both smiling down at the wet patch she had made on the sofa and as she blushed Amy bent back down again and kissed her on the lips, kneeling between her thighs as she pressed them together to try and hide her shame.

'You *squirted*,' Amy grinned.

Emilia shook her head, and closed her eyes again, too embarrassed to admit it.

'You did, and it was amazing,' said Celeste, her lips glistening in the moonlight.

Emilia tried to turn her head to the side to hide her face, but Amy clamped her palms on either cheek and drew her back.

'It's okay, it's nothing to be ashamed of.'

She opened her eyes briefly and blushed even harder as Amy nodded kindly at her.

'Did it feel good?'

Emilia took a deep breath, and then nodded very slowly. 'I just felt really relaxed.'

Amy laughed quietly, and kissed her again as Celeste squeezed her thigh. 'I told you, girls eat pussy better than boys.'

Emilia giggled sharply and Amy clamped her hand down over her mouth.

As she calmed down Amy looked down at her and grinned. She looked on, puzzled at her girlfriend's sudden change of expression, then watched with even more curiosity as she stood up and darted out of the room, leaving her and Celeste alone.

'Where is she going?' she said, bemused.

'I have no idea,' said Celeste, sitting up and looking toward the dark corridor.

She flopped back down on the couch a moment later and Emilia stroked Celeste's arm with her fingers, smiling across at her.

'Thank you,' she said quietly. 'That was beautiful.'

'It was. So are you.'

A moment later they both heard the pitter patter of naked feet on the tiles as Amy returned, holding something behind her back.

'Ok, you mustn't laugh,' she said, grinning and trying not to jump up and down. 'I bought this with me, and honestly I was terrified bringing it through baggage control.'

Emilia sat up, resting her hand between Celeste's bare thigh as she turned.

Amy's hands trembled as she revealed her little secret, holding it out in front of her with a mixture of embarrassment and excitement.

'Oh my goodness,' said Emilia, covering her mouth.

'Yes,' said Celeste. '*Fuck* yes.'

In her hands, Amy was holding an enormous skin coloured realistic dildo, connected to a harness.

'Is that a strap on?'

Amy nodded.

'Here,' said Celeste, releasing Emilia's fingers and standing up. 'Let me show you.'

She took the monstrous rubber cock out of Amy's hand and squeezed it, grinning. Then she loosened the straps and unbuckled the clips, sliding one side around Amy's tight little thighs and then coming around the front, obscuring her from Emilia's vision.

The pair of them giggled as she tightened the harness, then she stepped back and Emilia gasped. Amy wiggled her hips and the other two burst into laughter as the rubber cock flopped back and forth.

'Oh good grief,' said Amy. 'It's really heavy!'

She moved closer as Celeste knelt back onto the couch and slid up so she was straddling Emilia, her sumptuous breasts just inches from her mouth. Then she turned back and smiled.

'How's it feel?' she said as Amy knelt behind her.

'You tell me.'

Amy held the cock tight between her fingers, sliding them up and down it's length as she grinned. It felt strange against her skin, almost dusty, not soft, but not too hard either. She reached out and roughly pulled down Celeste's knickers with her free hand, sliding two fingers up and down her parting. Then she leaned forward and pressed the head against the girl's wet lips.

She watched as they parted, grinning as the shaft disappeared inside, listening as she moaned. Then she started to thrust.

Emilia reached up and pulled the gorgeous French girl down, kissing her lips as she was pushed back and forth by Amy. She gasped as Celeste's fingers closed over her breast and as she caressed her, she slid her own hand down between her legs. She reached up and grinned into her lips as she felt the material of the cock, sliding in and out of her along with the tips of Amy's fingers as she guided it back and forth. Then she worked her way around until she found their new friend's clit, and began to swirl.

Her reaction was immediate, moaning and arching her back up, pressing her breasts into Emilia's face and she squealed with delight as they enveloped her. She turned her head sideways and slipped a nipple into her mouth and Celeste cried out again.

They didn't care anymore if the boys heard them.

It didn't matter.

Not now.

Amy started to thrust harder, pushing her hips deeper and deeper as Celeste began to shake. The sight of the girl's bottom, her cheeks spread out before her made her feel naughty and she took one hand away from the big rubber cock and stroked her.

Then she pulled her hand away and brought it back down *hard*.

Celeste moaned as Amy spanked her, the crack echoing through the lounge.

The sensation was incredible, Emilia sucking her nipple and pressing against her clit, her pussy filled with Amy's strap on. The sweet pain as she struck her again.

Amy grinned and laughed, as she realised that this was what the men saw as they fucked them, and she *loved* it.

She swept her hand across the girl's bottom again, caressing it softly as Emilia sucked on her nipple, her fingers speeding up. She could feel her starting to cum, her breathing was changing and she was tightening her stomach.

Amy could sense it too, and she grinned as she thrust harder and harder, looking at the girl'a cute little bottom as she pushed her back and forth. Then she bit her lip in anticipation, and slid her finger down, pressing it softly against her sweet little hole.

Celeste came instantly.

She bucked and moaned so loud it boomed through the villa, shaking and shuddering, holding Emilia tight as she collapsed forward into her arms. Thrusting and writhing as she came, the sensation flowing through her.

Slowly and steadily, Amy pulled out and unclipped herself from the straps as Celeste slid down and lay to the side of her girlfriend. She dropped the rubber cock down to the side of the sofa, letting it fall to the floor as she too snuggled up next to them both.

For a while they just lay together, stroking each other and

snoozing as their breathing settled.

Feeling relaxed and safe, calm and gentle.

Then Amy looked up at Emilia, reticence clear on her face, even in the shadows of the night. 'If I lay down, will you do something for me?'

She looked shy as she spoke, almost ashamed and vulnerable. It was a rare look for her and Emilia's expression changed to a curious one as Celeste opened her eyes and glanced between them.

'Will you?' Amy hesitated, and then leaned back. 'Will you... put your tongue, *there* again?'

Emilia felt a taboo thrill shoot through her chest and spread out to her hips and legs and arms, like thick warm honey filling her veins.

Amy's face blushed as she stayed silent, then a moment later she started to shake her head in shame. 'It's okay, if you didn't like it before, we don't hav-'

Emilia nodded, smiling.

'I want to,' she said, reaching out to embrace her girl. 'I'd *like* to.'

They held each other for a little while, just breathing each other's scent, feeling each other's bodies shifting and wriggling.

'Lay on your back,' whispered Emilia softly into Amy's ear as she felt her begin to calm down.

Celeste sat up and shifted aside, letting Amy turn and lay down on her back, sliding her legs apart a little as Emilia looked around, quickly finding what she was searching for.

She tiptoed carefully across the living room tiles and picked up a large cushion from the chair opposite, then she shuffled back and lifted her girlfriend's bottom into the air, sliding the pillow underneath.

Amy blushed again and smiled sweetly as Emilia knelt down between her thighs. Celeste looked on, shifting around so she was sat by Amy's head, bristling with excitement as the two of them gazed at each other.

'I love you,' said Amy.

'I love you too.'

'You two are making me *melt*,' said Celeste, grinning wildly.

Emilia leaned forward and took Amy's nipple into her mouth, sucking on it gently, making her girl writhe beneath her and grabbing hold of her hair, pulling it as she arched her back and moaned.

Emilia could feel how wet she was against her hip as they moved together. Slowly and steadily she began to kiss her way down, inch by inch, one hand cupping her breast, Amy's fingers clasped over the top, the other teasing its way across her skin as Celeste cradled her rosy warm cheeks in the palms of her hands.

She heard Amy hold her breath as Emilia's lips hovered over her warmth, then she watched with wide eyes as she leaned forward and kissed her pussy.

Amy's hand reached up for Celeste, pulling her forward and moaning out loud as Emilia kissed her way slowly up and down, tasting her, teasing her. Then she slipped her tongue out of mouth and swirled it against her girl's soaking, parted lips, glancing up as her two embracing girls kissed.

Amy cried out, another echo resounding through the villa, making Emilia panic and move her tongue faster, swirling it smoothly as Amy's juices flooded her mouth.

As she did so, Amy arched up and squeezed the back of Emilia's head, gripping her face so tightly between her thighs that for a moment she struggled to breath.

As she relaxed her muscles, Emilia pulled back laughing and licking her lips, taking a breath and then settling forward again, sliding her wrist in front of her and spreading her wide open.

She pushed her finger inside now, just one at first, curling it towards her as she thrust.

Delicately, she began to tease her way down Amy's slit, all the way to the bottom where the little bridge of skin separated her pussy, from *there*.

Over and over again, she drew close. Just dabbing her tongue against her girl's skin and each time Amy would tense and then relax.

Then it was time.

She'd teased her long enough.

She arched her two fingers back and up, just as Celeste had done to her and began to thrust.

And then she pushed her girl's thighs further apart and tilted her back.

Finally, without any further hesitation, she slipped down and swirled the tip of her tongue against Amy's sweet little forbidden hole.

Her reaction was instantaneous.

She arched her back and shook, as though she was vibrating. It took all of Emilia's strength to hold her still, like a bucking bronco in a mid-western tavern. She held her firm and kept her fingers going, her tongue swirling as Amy cried out in silence and as Celeste held her arms.

Together they crashed back down onto the sofa as Amy's hushed cry became a long drawn out moan.

Emilia felt her fingers become slick as Amy's pussy swelled, writhing and shuddering as she started to come.

'Keep going,' she hissed, squeezing her thighs together against Emilia's face again as she curled her fingers tighter and pushed up, pulsing against her g-spot.

'Yes.'

Emilia pushed her tongue harder against Amy's little opening as her fingers fastened.

'*Yes, yes.*'

She began to pull harder now too, her fingers straining with the effort.

'*Yes.*'

Amy stretched her legs and shuddered.

'*Yes,*' her single word seemed to stretch out and morph into a long, quiet moan.

Then she twitched and Emilia felt a sweet tasting fluid gush over her lips as Celeste looked on, grinning wildly.

She gasped as Amy shook. Her whole body seemed to go ridged and then after a few seconds she flopped back down onto the sofa still held tight, as Emilia licked her lips.

For a while they all lay still as Amy twitched, squeezing her thighs and wriggling back and forth, just breathing and coming down, gradually settling as their heart rates slowed.

With great care Emilia crawled up beside them both, looping her arms around Amy's waist and pulling her in close, so her face was nuzzled into her neck, then she gently lifted her and rolled her over until she was on top of her, and Celeste was beside them both.

After a few moments, Amy's arms wrapped around Emilia's chest and shoulders.

'Thank you,' she whispered.

Emilia leaned down and kissed her on the forehead, sensing the subtle change in her breathing as she began to fall asleep.

For a little while, her and Celeste lay awake, enjoying each other's scent, listening to each other breathe, watching each other smile, and feeling their heart's beating through each other's skin and chest's.

She watched as the French girls eyes became heavier and heavier, eventually fluttering closed as she drifted off.

A year ago Emilia wouldn't have dreamed of doing the things she had done tonight, she would've paled at the thought of kissing another girl, let alone anything else. She would've been so utterly embarrassed and ashamed by the idea that she would've had to lay down. Meeting Amy and falling in love with her had opened a door to a beautiful new world. One that she was still struggling to come to terms with at times, but one that was filled with deliciously tempting and taboo pleasures, that were now impossible for her to resist.

The truth it seemed, was that she was more like her sister than she had ever realised before, and as she came to this realisation she smiled.

Tomorrow she would call her. It was time.

Her whole body felt like it was floating on a calm and soothing ocean of happiness, gently swaying her back and forth and rocking her off to sleep.

And after a while, she too closed her eyes, and smiled.

*

CHAPTER FIVE

The morning sun shone bright through the large double doors of the patio as Emilia and Amy slept soundly, wrapped in each other's arms. They were still laying together, naked on the sofa with a blanket pulled over them both when Mark woke up.

He smiled warmly as he walked through to the living room and stretched, glancing down at his two sleeping girls. Then he frowned and his eyes widened as he noticed the slumbering figure of Celeste, asleep in one of the armchairs, frowning as he pieced together the rather noisy events of last night.

It was already warm, even at this hour of the morning and he contemplated turning on the air conditioning, but he didn't want to risk waking them.

Instead he quietly slid the door open just less than a foot to let some outside freshness in and then tip toed over to the sofa and slid the blanket higher so it covered Amy's bare shoulders.

He looked at her for a moment in her sleep, then at Emilia, her eyes still closed, and smiled to himself again.

As quietly as he could, he crept back towards the kitchen and began to make breakfast.

Emilia stirred as the sound of the boiling kettle made its way through to the lounge. She was vaguely aware that Mark had been beside them, but it was fuzzy as though it might have been a dream.

Amy wasn't a dream though, she was real and sleeping soundly between her thighs, both of them naked beneath the blanket that covered them.

Tears came to her eyes for a moment as it crossed her mind that she'd never been happier. She loved Cassian with all her heart, but falling in love with Amy too had made her feel complete. It had changed all of her preconceptions of what love could be and shaken the foundations of her whole world, leaving it brighter and more beautiful every day.

Opening up her marriage with Cass had been the start of the greatest adventure she'd ever had.

She held Amy a little tighter as she took a deep breath through her nose, breathing in the girl's scent and feeling dizzy with love. She ran her fingers through a loose lock of her sweet red hair and closed her eyes again.

Last night had been incredible.

The three of them, making love together.

It had felt so different. So safe and so gentle.

And she'd *squirted*. Amy too.

She blushed at the thought and her chest filled with butterflies as the memory of the sensation came back to her.

Celeste's smooth tongue and her sweet little fingers had felt incredible. But it was Amy's electrifying touch and her soft, kind lips that had sent her over the edge. It was how Amy made her *feel*.

She made her feel *warm*.

Like drinking a hot chocolate on a cold winters night. Like being wrapped in a blanket in front of a roaring fire. When they were together, she couldn't help but smile as her insides kindled.

Amy was stirring.

Her fingers squeezed Emilia's skin as she woke up, her eyes squinting like a mole as she looked around.

'I was dreaming about us,' she said, mumbling softly.

'What was it about?'

'We were getting married on a boat out at sea,' she blushed as she said it, and then laughed quietly. 'Cass and Mark were there and they walked us down the aisle.'

Emilia kissed her on the forehead. 'Sounds amazing.'

'It was silly, the aisle was a bouncy castle and the priest was a dinosaur.'

'Now *that* sounds amazing.'

Amy looked around as the echo of footsteps on the tiled floor filled the room and a moment later, Mark reappeared carrying a tray of coffee and croissants, wearing just his boxers and a warm friendly smile. As he approached he lay Amy's silk gown down on the arm of the sofa, along with two big jumpers of his own.

'Morning,' he said, raising his eyebrows. 'How was your night?'

Emilia covered her face in embarrassment and tried to pull the blanket over herself as Amy laughed.

'It was alright.'

'Just alright? From what I heard, I'm going to have to up my game,' he said, putting down the tray in front of them as they laughed. 'Croissants and coffee for my favourite girls.'

Emilia's eyes widened and she melted a little.

Amy sat up and took hold of her gown, sliding it on as Mark leaned in. Emilia smiled as they kissed, Amy holding his cheek and grinning.

'Is Cass up?' she asked, suddenly missing him and feeling a little guilty as she glanced at the still sleeping figure of Celeste.

'I don't think so, I heard him mumbling a while ago but I think he was talking in his sleep. Want me to go check?'

'No, it's okay. Let him rest.'

Now that Amy was sitting upright Emilia wriggled around until her legs were free, proceeding to arrange herself with as much dignity as she could manage beneath the little blanket.

Her eyes darted around and she blushed at the sight of all of their clothes, strewn around the living room floor.

Amy passed her Mark's thin jumper as he picked up a garment which turned out to be her knickers. He dangled them on the end of his finger and winked at her, throwing them towards her with a grin before he sat down in one of the little arm chairs close to them.

She caught them, dropping the blanket and exposing herself. For a moment she panicked, and then she realised it didn't matter anymore.

Mark and Amy were family now. She didn't need to be embarrassed or uncomfortable. She didn't need to feel ashamed or silly.

Amy was right, it didn't matter what other people thought.

They were home.

She stood up and shimmied her knickers back on in front of them both, then she pulled on his jumper, enjoying his scent as it wrapped around her like a hug, before sitting back down, truly comfortable in her skin for the first time in a while.

She leaned forward and began to roll up a pancake as Celeste's eyelids began to flutter.

'*Mon Dieu*,' she whispered, looking around and smiling slowly as she tucked herself back under the covers.

'Bonjour chérie,' said Amy.

'I'm honoured,' laughed Celeste as she glanced at Mark and blushed.

'How did you sleep?' asked Emilia before she bit down on her now tightly rolled pancake.

Celeste took a deep breath and sighed, shaking her head. '*So* well.'

'Have a pancake,' said Mark, standing up. 'Coffee?'

'I'm in love with him already,' she said, winking at Amy as she nodded gratefully.

They ate quietly, relaxing and enjoying the warm air as it flowed in from outside through the open patio doors, the sunlight shimmering on the surface of the pool like flashing cameras on a red carpet.

'Do you want to go shopping together today?' said Amy, delicately dabbing her lips as she looked at Emilia and Celeste.

'I'd like that,' she smiled, nodding as Amy turned back towards Mark.

'I have to work this afternoon,' said Celeste, morose.

'Do you mind if we take the car? We can drop Celeste home and you and Cass can chill here for the day?'

'Sure,' he said. 'All day?'

'Probably,' said Amy, turning back to Emilia, who grinned.

'What time do you want to leave?' she asked, looking up at the clock which was showing half past eight. 'Do you need to get home at any time, Celeste?'

'By ten?'

'There's a market open just after that, near the Jardin?' said Amy, touching Emilia's arm. 'Is that okay?'

Emilia smiled and nodded, taking another bite followed by a sip of coffee.

'Quelle heure est-il?' said Celeste looking around

'Huit heures,' said Mark.

'Plenty of time for a *shower* then?' she said, raising her eyebrows and letting the end of her sentence dangle in proposition.

Mark's chest tightened and his breathing slowed, meeting Celeste's mischievous and suggestive gaze as Amy drank a gulp of coffee down.

Emilia had noticed the intonation too and after a moment she crossed her legs to conceal her sudden arousal, taking a wobbly breath as she looked to Celeste then Mark and then his wife.

'Of course you can. I'll go grab you a towel,' said Amy as she put her mug back down, oblivious of the looks being exchanged by the other three. 'You can use our room if Cass is still asleep, or...' she said, tailing off as she finally saw their faces. 'Oh.'

Celeste tilted her head sideways and shrugged, then she glanced at Emilia and spoke tentatively. 'Maybe we could, erm, see if your *mari* is awake too?

Emilia couldn't help but grin, flashing a smile and then biting her lip with excitement as she looked across at the other two.

Amy opened her mouth to speak but found she couldn't, closing it again before standing up suddenly and taking hold of Emilia's hand, pulling her upright and out of the room excitedly.

Celeste leapt up a second later, the blanket falling away as she pulled Mark's other jumper over her head, grinning as she caught him looking, then she bounded across the room in just a few steps, grabbing hold of his big hand in hers as they followed at a pace.

Emilia tried to keep up with Amy, giggling as they stopped at the door of Cassian's bedroom, pushing it open gently and peering in. She laughed as she saw the shape of her husband asleep in the darkness, spread out across the whole of their double bed, naked with the duvet wrapped loosely around his legs.

He was also sporting a rather impressive morning wood.

She turned and pulled Amy in, nodding for her to take a look and she gleefully peered into the room, letting her eyes adjust.

'Oh my, well *he's* ready,' she pulled back as Mark and Celeste caught up.

Emilia darted inside and slipped onto the bed beside her husband, leaning across and kissing him gently until he woke up. As he came to, he slipped his hands around her neck and pulled her close to him and she laughed.

'Hold that thought,' she said, pressing a finger to his lips. 'Come and join us in the shower.'

His eyes widened as he processed what she was saying, then he looked into the corridor and saw Celeste waving back at him and he blinked. A moment later he was stood up as Emilia handed him a little towel.

Dragging him along, she pushed open the door to the shower room with her foot and pulled him inside, with Amy, Celeste and Mark just behind them.

The big bathroom was huge.

It was a separate room from the little en-suite attached to their bedrooms, and was clearly designed with sharing in mind. Amy grinned as they walked in and Celeste's eyes went wide.

'Oh ça alors *c'est incroyable*,' she said as she took it all in, whilst Cassian stared on bewildered.

The room was divided by a floor to ceiling glass partition which could be entered from either side. Above them were two large, wide and flat shower heads, attached to the ceiling with separate digital temperature touch controls which glowed a gentle blue.

Amy stepped forward and untied the bow of her silk

gown, letting it slip to the floor, revealing her naked bottom. Then she tiptoed across and darted behind the dividing glass wall, turning both of the shower heads on and leaping back as cold water gushed out.

Emilia grinned and pushed past Mark, who bumped into Cassian as she pulled Celeste along with her.

'Come on,' she said as the two of them pulled Mark's jumpers off, over their head, throwing them on top of Amy's gown.

The two men watched as their wives embraced their stunning new young friend beneath the hot running water of the shower heads, their naked and wet bodies pressing together as they began to kiss and touch each other. Emilia still had her knickers on, now soaked through with water and almost translucent and they watched with wide eyed frozen expressions as the other two girls pulled them down with difficulty as they stuck to her thighs.

Cassian reacted first, dropping his towel and grinning back toward Mark as he hopped across the warm tiles and stepped in behind Amy, rubbing his hands over her warm, wet hips as Emilia kissed her mouth.

Mark shook his head, laughing as he walked in, pulling down his boxers and kicking them aside as he sidled up behind Emilia, spinning her around, his cock growing as Celeste watched wide eyed.

Amy pressed herself against Emilia's back, tucking her chin into her shoulder, blowing her husband a kiss as Cassian picked her up. She screamed and laughed with delight as he pressed her up against the glass partition, water cascading down their bodies as he bent down and thrust his head between her breasts, taking one nipple into his mouth and squeezing the other between his fingers.

Emilia giggled with delight as Mark kissed her, holding her tight against his raging manhood and thrusting it between her legs so she had to part her thighs. Not wanting Celeste to be left out, she reached out for her hand and grabbed it, pulling her closer until their wet bodies touched.

He was so thick.

She ached for him.

Thankfully he wasn't wasting any time. He spun her around and pushed her gently up against the glass so she was facing Celeste, inches from her face and so close they could kiss. Then he parted her legs wider and thrust himself inside her so fast and so hard that she squealed with joy.

She hadn't been expecting last night, or this morning. She had resigned herself to an early night followed by a lazy lie in, and later a coffee and a croissant whilst reading by the pool.

Instead she was already on the verge of orgasm, with Mark's thick cock buried deep in her pussy as Celeste's fingers slid across her breasts.

She looked down as Cassian knelt on the floor, his hands either side of Amy's slick thighs and she watched in delight as his mouth and tongue closed over her girlfriend's parting. The gushing water of the shower splashing over them both in a torrent.

Amy's head tilted back and she reached out, holding onto Celeste's arm as she moaned, Cassian's tongue sweeping across her clit as his fingers pushed and curled inside her. Steam swept around them all as the cascade of water warmed the room, filling their lungs and permeating their skin. It felt rejuvenating after the sweat and the heat of last night.

Emilia felt Mark's hand close around her breast and she turned as his chiseled jaw appeared on her shoulder. She leaned to kiss him and they moved together like an undulating wave as they made love. Her hand was pressed high up on the glass partition, whilst her other one was wrapped around the back of his neck as they worked in time together.

Then he thrust hard and pulled out and she felt him move sideways and sweep Celeste around. She froze, looking up into his eyes as his firm arms gripped her hand and slid down her back, then she turned and looked at Amy who caught her eye in between moans and nodded.

Mark spun her around now too, her hands sliding up the glass partition, the water splitting at her touch and flowing past and over her fingers as she slowly parted her thighs and looked sideways, grinning at Emilia who placed a delicate hand hand over hers and squeezed.

Celeste sensed movement between her legs and giggled, her excitement palpable and then Emilia watched her expression change, her jaw dropping and her eyes closing as Mark's cock penetrated her.

'Oh *putain*, il est si épais. *Thick.*'

Cassian stood up and Emilia watched as Amy wrapped her arms around his muscular shoulders, her little frame dwarfed by his huge stature. He picked her up by her bottom and she jumped onto his waist as he pressed her back up against the glass and kissed her hard.

A moment later she moaned into his neck as his long cock slipped inside her easily and he began to thrust so hard and fast that Emilia felt the partition wobble.

'Oh *yes*,' said Amy, reaching out for Celeste's other hand. They grasped each other and pressed their fingers together against the waterfall running down the shaking divider as Emilia circled behind them both, feeling the shape of Mark's behind, running her fingers up his spine as he thrusted into the little French girl, and then across to her own husband's familiar muscles and ridges.

Celeste cried out as Mark grew inside her, listening to his wife moan, becoming thicker and making her feel full as he throbbed. It felt so good, the warm water rushing over her skin as she squeezed Amy's fingers. She turned her head and caught Emilia's eye.

'I want you,' she said, reaching out for her and pulling her close, kissing her as Mark fucked her harder and harder with Emilia now pressed between them all. She felt Celeste's hand slide down her stomach and press into her pussy and she moaned into her mouth. Then Mark moved and took hold of her once more, pushing her legs apart as Celeste guided him in.

Amy watched and then whispered to Cassian who lowered her down and smiled as she leaned across and kissed Celeste. The two of them fell back against the partition as their fingers found each other. Then Cassian took ahold of Celeste's hips and slipped inside her.

It was incredible.

'I love you,' said Emilia, turning to Amy as Mark thrust harder and harder.

'I love you too,' moaned Amy, her voice uneven as Cassian ravished the little French girl.

'I'm going to cum.'

'So am I,' said Amy, even louder as she dug her free hand into Celeste's back.

They came together, each one spurring on the other with their pleasure as their orgasms built and then spilt over the edge. The men pumping into them, filling them up, their fingers working each other, their knees buckling as they thrust and strained.

Then they all went silent.

Mouths open.

Eyes closed.

Fingers touching.

The girls fell into one another as their husbands eased off, holding each other and kissing, breathing and caressing as they came down, letting the water wash over them, the steam rolling across their skin as the men leaned against the partition, recovering.

Emilia and Amy sank down onto the floor of the shower, pulling Celeste with them, their wet naked bodies pressed together as the men tried to stay upright.

Mark started to laugh as he caught his breath. 'I think I'm going to need another shower.'

'I think we all might,' said Cassian, his cock still hard and throbbing.

'We may never get out of here then,' said Amy, looking up at them both, her hair clinging to her face as the water ran down it in little rivulets.

Mark laughed and stroked his cock, bringing it back to life as Cassian did the same.

'We're supposed to be going shopping,' laughed Emilia as Amy kissed her again, sliding her hand between her thighs. 'And you're supposed to be going to work.'

'It's okay,' said Celeste, sliding her hand up higher than Amy's as Emilia closed her eyes and gasped. 'We can be a little late.'

*

The underground car park was well lit, clean and clever. Unlike any that Emilia had parked inside back in Oxford, or any city in the whole of England for that matter.

The tyres of the hire car gently squealed as they glided across the smooth surface of the concrete. Each bay was large enough to comfortably fit any size of family vehicle instead of being crammed together like sardines, with passengers struggling to open doors without hitting the vehicle next to them.

The best part was the red and green lights above each space. Red meant the space was in use, and green meant it was free. This simple mechanic made finding a space quick, efficient and easy and she imagined it would reduce frustration and congestion at busy times.

Amy quickly navigated round to a clear spot and pulled up, and a moment later they were all out and heading towards the nearest lift. There appeared to be several dotted around and Emilia was impressed with how clean, fast and responsive they were.

They stepped inside and the door swished shut and a moment later she watched the carpark disappear. Her jaw dropped open as the lift rose up out of the ground and came to a smooth halt in the middle of a stunning park.

All around them, visible through the glass walls of the lift, were lush green trees, stone terraced walls and seats, little man-made rivers through which ran clear water, and hundreds of people milling around in the warm sunshine of the day.

It was beautiful.

'It's quite something, isn't it?' said Celeste, squeezing her hand as the doors slid open. Emilia and Amy stepped out and turned around, slowly taking in the panorama.

'Et regarde, over there.'

A few hundreds yards away stood the imposing, curved stone walls of the Colosseum.

It was easy to imagine what it would have been like to see almost two thousand years ago, as it inspired the same sense of trepidation, excitement and intimidation now for Emilia as it must have done then.

She pictured herself amongst the gladiators as they prepared for battle, their dark lean torso's, their ripped muscles, their grizzled expressions, their fear and sweat. She licked her suddenly dry lips and secretly wondered if there were any naughty gladiator books she could find on her e-reader.

'This is where we *partie*,' said Celeste, shrugging.

Amy smiled at her and took a deep breath. 'Can we see you again?'

'I was hoping you would say that.'

Emilia grinned and laughed. 'Can we have your number?'

'Give me your phone,' she said as Emilia plucked it out of her bag.

She bristled with excitement as Celeste typed it in, then she handed it back and smiled. 'Call me.'

Amy nodded and then reached out to kiss her on the cheek. Emilia watched as they did so, three times and then a fourth. Then Celeste turned to her and did the same.

For a moment they all held hands and then Celeste let go and turned away. 'A tout alors, belles filles. Ne m'oublie pas.'

They waved as she walked away, eventually disappearing behind a row of trees in the distance.

'So when can we see her again?' laughed Amy as she turned back to Emilia.

'Shall we book her a flight for next week?'

The two of them laughed as they began to walk toward the colosseum.

'I really enjoyed last night,' said Amy. 'And this morning.'

'Me too,' said Emilia. 'I like playing with you.' Their fingers brushed together as they walked, their dresses swaying back and forth in the gentle breeze. 'It's liberating. I feel like anything is possible.'

'I know what you mean.'

The city centre was an architectural mixture of historical buildings, neon lights, eighties design aesthetic and ultra-modern glass-fronted facades.

The two of them walked side by side, marvelling at the eclectic blend of cultures and periods as they weaved their way through tight lanes, milling tourists and brightly coloured market stalls.

After a while Amy stopped to admire a necklace at one, jumping as Emilia's hand stroked the small of her back lightly.

'Isn't it beautiful?' she said, looking up at the stall holder as Emilia nodded. 'Combien?'

'Cent cinquante euros,' came the quick reply.

'Voulez-vous en prendre cent trente?'

Emilia frowned as the stall holder grunted and then nodded reluctantly.

Amy dug into her cleavage, sliding her hand into her money pouch that she had strapped around her chest, hidden beneath her dress, and removed the correct amount, passing it to the vendor who snuffled it away on his person. Then she gestured for Emilia to turn around.

'Hold up your hair,' she said as Emilia gasped.

Amy unclipped the little necklace and reached up, draping it round her girlfriend's neck and then clipping it in place.

'Let me see,' she said as she turned back round.

'I love it,' said Emilia, admiring the little pendant and stroking the silver chain.

She leaned forward to kiss Amy but stopped part way and faltered, feeling awkward.

Amy's expression changed in an instant, frowning and hurt.

'You don't want to kiss me in public?'

'No, I do,' said Emilia, starting to feel even more silly. 'I just, we haven't done that before.'

'You've licked my ass,' pouted Amy, laughing now. 'Twice. But a kiss in front of a bunch of foreigners, that you may never see again, is a step too far?'

'No. Yes. I don't know. I'm sorry.'

Amy shook her head. 'Fine,' she said. 'How about we start by holding hands?'

Emilia smiled, relieved. 'I can manage that.'

Amy reached out her hand and wiggled her fingers.

Emilia looked down at them, then back up at Amy's raised eyebrows and laughed. Still a little hesitantly, she reached out and tingled as their fingers interlocked.

Amy smiled and turned, walking slowly along past more stalls in silence as they enjoyed the sensation of being together, proudly in public.

Emilia played with her new necklace idly as they walked, looking down at it from time to time.

'Do you like it?' said Amy.

'I love it. It's from you.'

*

The street widened ahead as they stepped out onto a broad avenue. Together they crossed over into the middle of a huge two way system, through the centre of which was a pedestrianised area. As they walked along they passed little ponds of water in shallow concrete pools and fountains that spurted up out of tiny holes. Children played among them in little swimming costumes, running in and out of the spray as they giggled and laughed with delight.

Emilia smiled as she watched them, squeezing Amy's hand a little tighter each time they passed a family playing together.

At the far end of the boulevard, the road stopped and together they crossed over a simple bridge leading into a wide and quiet park.

The garden was beautiful and bigger than she had imagined. Weaving and meandering through it was a series of stone built channels within which clear water flowed freely into larger, darker reservoirs where green and white lily pads floated.

Together they leaned over the stone railing of one and

looked down into the water, watching as hundreds of large fish swam and milled around through the little archways and tunnels below, occasionally flapping or gulping at the surface before disappearing again into the depths.

The area they stood in was lined with large trees providing welcome shade above lush green grass and gravel walk ways.

It was beautiful and relaxing, despite being full of hundreds of people and tourists from all walks of life. If Amy listened carefully she could hear French, German, Swedish and occasionally English being spoken amongst the groups of people sat in the shade beneath the canopy.

After a while they moved on from the water and held hands again, swaying gently as they walked beside one another.

Emilia was too excited to talk. She once again felt like she was back at school, holding Cassian's hand for the first time as they were walking with their friends. She felt giddy with pride, and she noticed lots of different people smiling at them as they meandered along the river side.

It was wonderful.

They stopped after a while at a little park cafe and ordered two lattes, sitting down in the shade of an old tree and holding hands across the table.

'Thank you,' said Emilia.

'What for?'

'For being patient with me.'

'That's okay,' she said, stroking the back of her hand.

'This is just all new to me, I've not been with a girl before. Well, I've not been with anyone but Cass before, but you know what I mean.'

Amy smiled and looked down at her coffee, blushing as Emilia frowned.

'Wait,' she said suddenly, seeing Amy's expression. 'Have *you* been with a girl before?'

Amy laughed and turned away as Emilia's eyes widened. She gasped and drew one hand to her mouth. 'You have!'

Amy shook her head in embarrassment, she was even glowing a little as she tried to hide from Emilia's searching eyes.

'Who? When?' she said. 'What was her name?'

'Ok, but you have to promise not to get upset. It was a fling, not a relationship,' she blushed again before saying quietly. 'I'm in love with you.'

'So it was just sex?'

Amy laughed. 'Her name was Melanie and I knew her at University, we lived together in halls.' She looked down at the table again and then back up at Emilia.

'That's it?'

'You want the full story?'

'Yes,' said Emilia, visibly excited.

'You are so weird,' laughed Amy.

'Does Mark know?'

Amy nodded. 'It used to be one of his favourite bedtime stories.'

Emilia giggled with delight.

'We met on moving-in day, but nothing happened at first, we were just friends. She was very cool, a year older than the rest of us after she'd taken a gap year to go travelling, so she was more mature and although it's funny to look back on now, she came across as wiser too. She'd *been places*, man.'

Amy rolled her eyes a little as she talked.

'She would always have a story to tell and they would be so wild and adventurous, kind of like Mark come to think of it, and usually they would end up with her shagging some gorgeous foreign man, that she would describe as looking somewhere between a film star and a supermodel. It was probably all bullshit, but we lapped it up. The rest of us had come straight up from college and although some of us had plans to travel after studying, the closest any of us had experienced to her adventures were family holidays to a handful of slightly more exotic places than Berlin or Barcelona.'

She paused to sip her coffee.

'About eight weeks in, I was studying late, the light must have been visible under my door, and I hear this knock, really gentle, but quite insistent and then Melanie's voice, whispering. So I get up, and I'm literally wearing a tank top and knickers and these awesome bed socks, and I go to the door and open it a crack and she's standing there in floods of tears.'

Emilia frowned and stopped stroking Amy's palm for a moment.

'Keep doing that,' said Amy, smiling. 'It feels nice.'

'Why was she crying?'

'Turns out she had a long distance boyfriend, some guy she'd met on her travels, and he'd dumped her via an email. She asked if she could come in and I don't think I actually said yes, but in she came and she just started unloading. They'd fallen in love in Vietnam, he was German but he spoke perfect English, he was five years older than her and was studying Ancient Cultures in Berlin, they were going to marry in Indonesia and buy a house boat in Sweden. All this history just flooded out of her like a gushing torrent. It was a whole new side to her that I'd never seen before.'

She smiled, reminiscing.

'You liked her?'

Amy nodded.

'I liked the real her, not the person she tried to be to impress everyone. We all did it, we all bigged ourselves up, exaggerated and embellished our past. Some people I'm sure made up whole new lives for themselves. University can be a big red reset button for some people I guess. But when her barriers fell down it confused the shit out of me.'

She laughed.

'There I was, consoling this stunning, older girl on my bed, dressed in my little tank top and knickers, doing my best to comfort her as she bawls her eyes out and I'm just really fucking aroused.'

Emilia's eyes grew wide and she giggled.

'Honestly, it was like the harder she cried, the wetter I got. Eventually I was too afraid to stand up.'

'Oh my goodness. What did you do?'

Amy bit her lip.

'I kissed her,' she said, smiling. 'I just leaned across and kissed her. At first she didn't react, she just sort of froze, and so did I. Then her lips moved and parted a little, and I felt her tongue against mine, and then her hand on my hip, and before I knew it we were naked under my duvet.'

She widened her eyes at Emilia and giggled, stroking and squeezing her hand.

'So what happened? Did you break up?'

'No, we're still together. I'm a serial bigamist, Em.'

Emilia slapped her hand lightly.

'Yes of course we did,' she laughed. 'Well, sort of. We never really got together as such, but it lasted a long time. We were on and off for about a year. I had a boyfriend for a little while, but when that went wrong I ended up back with her. Sometimes we would sleep together if one of us was having a hard time. It was like we were each other's solace.'

Emilia nodded.

'It was the same thing each time, she would knock on my door, come in and have a cry, and then we would kiss. Or it would be me, knocking on her door. Honestly it got the point where if I saw or heard someone cry it would be an instant turn on. *Sploosh*.'

She laughed and wiped a tear from her eyes.

'It made me realise that I wasn't *strictly* straight, that I was somewhere on the spectrum, but the needle wasn't pointing exclusively at men.'

'What happened to her?'

'She got married to a guy named Aaron and they live on a houseboat on the Thames.'

'Do you still talk?'

'Sometimes,' Amy shrugged, then she smiled mischievously. 'We last met up around three years ago. Before Mark and I married.'

Emilia giggled and raised her eyebrows. 'Did you have a cry?'

'We had a cry.'

'You know I did study Drama at college,' laughed Emilia. 'I used to be pretty good at turning on the waterworks.'

'Don't joke,' said Amy.

Emilia sniffed a little and her eyes began to water.

Amy bit her lip as she shook her head. 'I'm warning you. I will come *right* here. It's like I'm conditioned.'

Emilia laughed and wiped her eyes and then leaned back in her chair as her girlfriend relaxed.

'You're so funny, I love it.'

'Wait, the other day,' said Emilia suddenly, her eyes wide. 'When I was crying just before Cass arrived. Were you?'

Amy started laughing and covered her mouth. 'Sploosh.'

'Oh my goodness!'

'Why do you think I was so desperate to get back to the villa?'

'You are sick.'

Emilia felt strangely reassured as they walked back towards the old city lanes, hand in hand again. There was a part of her that was sad that she wasn't Amy's first but it also meant that this wasn't just a passing curiosity, and like her - well almost like her - Amy was bi-sexual and comfortable with it. Wanting to hold hands wasn't just for show or for some sense of validation, it wasn't to convince herself of her feelings.

It was real.

As they reached the edge of the park, Emilia stopped. There was something she had to do. There was no point putting it off any longer. It wasn't something she could avoid. Amy turned to look at her and frowned.

'I'm sorry. I need to make a phone call.'

Amy nodded and smiled. 'Of course, I'll wait for you by the fountain.'

'Thank you.'

Amy stared for a moment longer, smiling kindly. 'She loves you. You know that right?'

'I know.'

'They both do.'

'I know.'

'Good luck.'

'Thank you.'

Amy turned and kept walking, crossing the road and disappearing behind a line of trees as Emilia watched.

She slipped her phone out of her handbag and unlocked it, glancing briefly at the photo of all four of them from the gorge two days ago before opening up her contacts and sliding down a little way. She held her finger on her sisters name, pausing and thinking. Then she pressed the call button and held the phone up to her ear.

It rang twice and Alice answered.

'Hey *thister*,' came her familiar voice. 'I can't believe you never told him you used to have a lisp.'

'I can't believe you fucked my husband over the dining room table, after I *specifically* told you not to.'

'Touché little Em,' she laughed down the line. 'I wondered when you were going to call.'

'I've missed you.'

'I wasn't expecting you to say *that*.'

'I'm sorry, I should've called you earlier.'

'Or texted, or checked in, but as you said, I did fuck your husband over your dining room table. I wasn't expecting much.'

'And our bed.'

'*And* in your bed.'

'How's the house?'

'Actually, I don't know. I'm in Berlin.'

'Berlin?'

'Yes, you know. The Opera House? The wall? Deutsche Bank.'

'I see,' said Emilia.

'How's Cass?'

'He's good, I think he was rather hoping you'd be at home when we got back.'

'Yeah, I promised him I'd let him fuck my ass.'

'*Alith!*' said Emilia, falling back into her old habit. 'Alice. *Fuck.*'

'Oops.'

She stayed silent for a while.

'I'm sorry,' her sister sounded genuine.

'You don't have to be.'

'I love you, you know?'

'Cassian keeps telling me that too.'

'We do though.'

'I know.'

'Are we going to be okay?'

Emilia smiled and took a deep breath. 'Always.'

'You're such a bitch.'

'A *perfect* little bitch, thank you very much.'

Alice laughed. 'You really are.'

'I've got to go, Amy is waiting.'

'When do I get to meet her?'

'Whenever you like.'

'Really? I thought maybe you might have a restraining order put on the two of us.'

'No, I trust you.'

Alice sniffed. 'That means a lot.'

'When will you be back from Germany?'

'For another ride? As soon as I've finished up here. Maybe a week?'

'I'll let him know. At least now I know what to get you for your birthday.'

'A big bottle of lube?'

'A big bottle of lube,' she nodded and laughed.

'Take care, Em.'

Emilia smiled. 'I love you, Al. Be careful.'

'I love you too.'

She took the phone away from her ear and ended the call, placing it back in her bag and pushing away from the bridge. She took a deep breath, enjoying the rich fresh air of the park one more time before she left to find Amy, closing her eyes and turning around, stretching her arms up into the air and then relaxing.

As she did so, she felt her shoulders drop as days of built up tension finally left her body. She opened her eyes again and smiled.

Everything was going to be okay.

She was going to make sure of it.

And she knew how now.

She turned around and almost skipped back towards where she last saw Amy.

As she approached she slowed down, watching her from a distance. She was talking to a little girl, holding a small ball out that had rolled up to her feet where she was sitting. As Emilia watched, she handed it back and smiled as the girl spoke and nodded, then she waved as she ran away.

For a fleeting moment she recognised the look on Amy's face and she grinned.

As she walked towards her, Amy got up and opened her arms wide for a hug.

'How did it go?'

'As well as can be expected with Alice,' she laughed. 'No, that's not fair. It went really well.'

'Are you okay?'

'I am,' she said. 'And for the first time in a few days, I really mean it.'

Amy reached up and kissed her, surprising her. For a moment she froze and then she realised she didn't care and she kissed her back, holding her tight in her arms and smiling as their lips pressed against each other. She pulled away and took hold of Amy's hand, and the two of them turned and followed their footsteps back towards the lanes, walking happily in silence and swinging back and forth.

Amy led the way, seemingly knowing her way around the city, walking with confidence and ease.

As they continued meandering they rounded another tight alleyway and as they did so, Amy gasped and squeezed Emilia's hand, pointing ahead.

'Look!'

She followed her gaze, her eyes widening as she saw what her girlfriend was pointing at.

An erotic boutique.

'We *have* to go in.'

Emilia stood open mouthed, blushing and suddenly filled with anxiety.

'Come on,' said Amy, dragging her excitedly towards the entrance.

*

* * *

The doorway was covered with a deep, thick red curtain and Emilia grimaced as Amy parted it to allow them through, pushing open the old wooden door frame behind it, a bell chiming as they stumbled through.

The inside was illuminated by low level lighting which gave the impression of a boudoir. Everywhere were deep blacks and shades of red, comfortable seats, leather sofas and shelves of neatly laid out and carefully arranged sex toys.

Emilia blanched as she glanced at a naked mannequin sporting an enormous strap on dildo around her waist, her mind flashing back to last night. Another was dressed in leather, a bull whip in one hand, a paddle in the other and a vibrating cock ring around its huge, erect silicone penis.

She wanted to laugh, turn around and run at the same time but Amy's grip was vice-like as she pulled her further into the little boutique.

A young girl behind a tall counter smiled sweetly at them both as they giggled and then went back to reading her book.

At the far end were a few more female mannequins dressed in stunning lace lingerie.

'Why don't we surprise the boys?' said Amy, mischievously.

She began to rifle through the assorted underwear until she gasped and pulled one set off the shelf. She turned and held it up to Emilia who blushed as she looked down at the almost non-existent garment.

Amy shook her head. 'No, too skimpy. How about... you find something for me, and I'll find something for you?'

Emilia looked back at the young girl behind the counter, still engrossed in her book and then turned back and nodded.

'Ok,' she said quietly.

She'd never been in a shop like this before. She'd bought and worn lingerie on many occasions. More so recently than ever before, but she'd always done it online and even then she'd created a separate email address, just so the order confirmations didn't appear in her regular email and cause her to go bright red every time she needed to email her mum.

She was always paranoid that one day she would send something from the wrong one, but she was ultra-careful and kept both email addresses in separate apps on her phone. At one point she'd even considered buying another phone altogether but decided that Cassian would think she was either cheating or a drug dealer and stopped herself.

As she began to browse her way down the aisle, the idea crossed her mind that this might be some sort of test.

Could she choose something that Amy would like? Did she know her well enough? Were they compatible? She thought back to all the times that Cassian had bought her underwear and how he must have felt. She wondered if he had browsed in one of these shops, picking up vibrators and dildos, chatting with the pretty staff, or had he just gone online and ordered whatever he liked the look of in some discount sale.

She laughed nervously under her breath and Amy glanced up at her from across the aisle.

'How are you getting on?'

Emilia shrugged. 'I've not found anything ye- Oh, wait.'

Her eyes fell across a stunning halterneck, semi-sheer, red lace basque with a deep plunge neckline, matching crotchless knickers and four dangling suspender straps, complete with sheer stockings. It was as though it was made for Amy.

She tingled as she picked it up and then grinned so wide as she held it that Amy couldn't resist and Emilia laughed as she ran excitedly around the corner to come and see.

'Mrs Black,' she said laughing as she approached. 'You have excellent taste.'

'Do you like it?'

'Do *you* like it?'

'I'd like to see you in it.'

'Shall we go and try it on?'

Emilia's face turned white. 'Here? Now?'

Amy nodded and grabbed the garment and Emilia's hand, pulling her along towards the back of the store to a little changing room with a thick black curtain. They rushed inside and pulled it across, then turned and giggled at one another.

Amy spun round and began to unbutton her dress, one by one. Emilia felt dizzy as she watched, smiling and feeling warm as Amy slid the straps off her shoulder and let it fall to the ground.

Quickly, she unclipped her bra and dropped it aside and then pulled down her knickers so she was stark naked. For a moment they both looked at each other in the floor length mirror, their eyes lingering, then Amy picked up the red lace lingerie and began to slip it on.

Emilia tied the lace that tucked in neatly against her lower back and Amy adjusted the chest, then she bit her lip and looked herself up and down.

'What do you think?'

Emilia tried to speak, but found that she couldn't, instead she just blushed and tried not to giggle.

'Well, I think we've found the right one for me,' laughed Amy, peeling it off again and letting it fall to the floor. 'I wonder if it will have the same effect on our husbands?'

She picked up her knickers and bra and slipped them back on, then pulled up her dress as Emilia watched closely.

'Your turn now,' said Amy, whipping the curtain open. 'Stay here, get naked and I'll come back with something.'

She winked as Emilia stood open mouthed inside the little cubicle and then she swished it shut and stalked away.

She wasn't sure what to do.

She wanted to play along, but she felt awkward. What if someone else came to the curtain and opened it? What if they saw her there, naked?

She was shaking with a mixture of excitement and fear, too anxious to move, paralysed with anxiety, then she made up her mind.

Steadily, trying desperately to calm her nerves, she unzipped her little summer dress and let it fall to the floor, pushing it to one side with her foot, then she undid her bra and covered her breasts with one arm, then finally she shimmied down her knickers.

She could hear footsteps approaching fast, and she panicked.

The curtain flew open.

'Qu'est ce que tu fais ici?'

Emilia almost screamed, but then she saw that it was Amy, with a huge grin on her face.

'Je suis désolé,' she said as she slipped back inside, Emilia doing her best to cover herself up with her hands.

'I hate you,' she hissed. 'I thought you were the girl out front, I nearly peed myself.'

Amy laughed, trying to stop herself from falling into hysterics.

'I'm sorry, I'm so sorry, I couldn't resist.'

'You're *so* mean.'

'I'm sorry. Here, look, I thought this might work.'

She handed the garment to Emilia and smiled, raising her eyebrows suggestively.

It was exactly the same one that Emilia had found for Amy, except this one was white.

Emilia grinned and looked back at her, nodding.

Tonight was going to be *fun*.

*

CHAPTER SIX

In contrast to Mark, Amy's driving was steady and calm, accelerating and breaking gently, taking corners and bends smoothly and even remaining on their side of the road most of the time.

As the sun began to set, Amy drew the car up slowly toward the gate and grinned as it began to open at their presence, glancing across at Emilia beside her and reaching out to squeeze her hand.

'I loved being out with you today,' she said as she pulled forward.

'Me too,' said Emilia. 'It was nice holding your hand.'

Amy smiled and nodded as she continued. 'I wonder what the boys have been up to?'

'They've probably been asleep all afternoon,' Amy laughed. 'We must have exhausted them by now.'

Emilia listened to the crunch of the tires on the gravel as Amy rolled to a stop. She switched off the engine and the noise of the air con ceased, leaving them in silence. The residual heat of the day immediately began to warm the car as the girls looked at one another in the failing light.

'This whole week,' said Emilia, blushing as she paused. 'I've never felt this way before.'

Amy smiled and reached across. 'Me neither. It's been really special.'

'I don't want to go home,' she said suddenly. 'I want our life to be like this, always.'

Amy laughed softly and looked down at their hands, clasped together tight over the central column.

'I'm serious,' she continued. 'I don't want to be away from you.'

'That crazy-hot scale's creeping back up.'

Emilia laughed and looked across at the Villa, frowning. Something was different but she couldn't put her finger on it.

'I want that too,' said Amy. 'But we have lives and jobs and family. It can't be like this every day.'

'I know, but this week,' she paused, struggling to find the right words. 'With everything that's happened. I'm stronger with you. It's made me realise that I want…' She tailed off.

'What do you want?'

'It's silly.'

'You can tell me.'

Emilia looked back at the villa, as it finally clicked. 'Why are the lights off?'

Amy frowned and looked up.

'That's odd.'

'The shutters are open too.'

'We're coming back to this conversation,' said Amy as she popped her door open and stepped out onto the gravel. 'Don't think you can distract me that easily Mrs Black.'

Emilia smiled and whispered to herself as Amy closed the door. 'Mrs Hamilton-Black.'

She took a deep breath and pulled the internal handle, pushing the smooth door open wide and stepping out onto the crunching gravel.

Amy was looking around confused and then she shrugged.

'Maybe they've gone out?'

'For a walk?'

Amy headed around to the back of the car as Emilia started to walk towards the entrance.

As she approached the front door, it opened.

She frowned and looked back at Amy who was still unloading shopping from the boot. Turning back, she found Cassian had appeared in the frame, and as she made eye contact with him, he bowed.

He was dressed in a midnight blue suit. It wasn't one she recognised. It was fitted, tucked and nipped in just the right places and it made him look devilishly handsome. His beard was trimmed neatly, his hair was cut short and combed.

He looked like a Prince.

She was so taken aback that she stopped walking altogether and stared, causing Amy to bump into the back of her and drop several bags onto the gravel.

'Em, what are you doi-? Oh,' she said as she saw movement and looked up to see Mark, standing next to Cassian, dressed from head to toe in a black dinner suit with a bow tie tucked neatly around his neck. In his hands he held two flute glasses.

The light behind them seemed to flicker oddly and as Amy looked past them she realised it was candlelight.

Dotted all around the entrance hall, along the edges of the walls, on top of the little table and around the edges of the sconces were maybe fifty or sixty tea candles, flickering in the darkness. It was beautiful and heart meltingly romantic.

The boys had been busy.

'Welcome home, ladies,' said Cassian, opening the door

wide as Mark offered them the champagne flutes. In the background, Emilia saw the bottle sitting in a bucket of ice.

She found her feet once again and stepped forward, gracefully taking the glass from Mark's fingers and turning to Cassian, a quizzical expression on her face.

'You'll find appropriate evening attire in our room,' said Cassian to both of them. 'If you would care to dress and then join us for a buffet dinner in the garden. The service will begin in fifteen minutes.'

'This is amazing,' said Amy, looking up at Mark who grinned back at her. 'You did all this?'

'You wait, you haven't seen half of it yet,' he said, winking at Cassian.

She turned back to Emilia and jumped up and down on the spot with excitement, her eyes wide with glee and anticipation.

'Come on, let's go get dressed,' she said, grabbing hold of her girlfriend's hand and heading off toward the bedroom.

Inside there were more candles, spaced out along the side dresser. Amy gasped as Emilia stepped in behind her.

'Look,' she said, pointing towards the bed. Laid out neatly across the duvet were two beautiful dresses and on the floor, two pairs of matching shoes.

'Oh my goodness,' said Emilia.

On the far side laid out for Amy, was a beautiful, intricate red lace, floor length, figure hugging evening dress with an open back and a long slit to the thigh. Closer to them both, laid out for Emilia, was a black lace, halterneck evening dress with a plunging neckline, a long thick silk belt and again, a thigh high split.

Both outfits were stunning, and by the look of them, perfectly sized.

Amy moved slowly across the room admiring both, occasionally glancing back at Emilia as their eyes glistened.

'They're beautiful,' she said, quietly.

'Where did they get them from?' said Emilia, picking up hers gently between her fingers.

'*When* did they get them?'

'Do you think they smuggled them here all the way from home?'

Amy laughed as she picked up her own and held it up to herself, letting the long trail drop to the floor by her feet.

'The lingerie,' said Amy suddenly, looking up.

'Oh my goodness, *yes*,' said Emilia turning around and picking up the shopping bag from the floor. She upended it on the bed watching as the two luxury boxes came tumbling out.

Amy grabbed hers and excitedly started to unbutton herself, almost jumping up and down on the spot with excitement. Emilia stretched across the bed and unboxed hers, admiring the way it was presented, then she began to strip too.

The girls helped each other dress and a few minutes later, they stood looking at themselves and each other in the mirror.

'This fits perfectly,' said Amy. 'Do you think they measured us in our sleep?'

'You look amazing.'

'So do you.'

Amy laughed and opened the door for Emilia, who blushed and smiled and then stepped through into the corridor. At the far end stood Cassian and Mark, holding a single red rose each, illuminated only by candlelight. She felt butterflies in her tummy immediately as she looked upon them and she turned back and took hold of Amy's hand for support as her girlfriend stood proudly by her side.

It was like being back at her prom again, except this time she had three dates.

Together they walked towards their husbands, feeling

beautiful and smiling uncontrollably. Emilia couldn't help but imagine what it might be like if they could all marry one another. She thought it might not be far off from this.

The men stepped apart, each one offering an arm to his wife and kissing them on the cheek.

'You look amazing,' said Cassian to Emilia. 'So does Amy.'

Mark nodded, as Emilia flashed a smile at him. The thought of them both looking like Greek god's flitted through her mind again.

'Would you care to join us for dinner?' said Cassian, gesturing towards the doorway to the living room. Emilia nodded, giddy with excitement. As he guided her through, her jaw dropped open.

'Oh my goodness,' said Amy, a few steps behind her as they drew level.

The large patio doors were wide open and on the wooden decking next the pool sat a large, dressed table with a white cover, four old wooden chairs and a selection of sumptuous food which looked at a glance like a banquet.

All around the garden were dotted tealight candles, shimmering in the darkness like a sea of flames. There was even a path through them, wide enough for all of them to walk.

The pool was also alight with more than a hundred candles floating in the gently lapping water, bumping and moving around. It must have taken them an hour alone just to light them all.

But beyond that, and the real reason that both Emilia and Amy had stopped in their tracks and were now beginning to grin and laugh, was the bed on the lawn.

It was the king size monster from Mark and Amy's room, but the men had erected a frame around it and draped sheer material down either side, leaving the top open to the star lit sky. It looked like a four poster romantic retreat on a tropical island.

'This is amazing,' said Amy quietly, shaking her head in wonder. She turned around and looked at Mark, her face a mixture of emotions as she smiled and tried to hold back tears at the same time. 'This is so beautiful.'

Emilia felt Cassian's hands wrap around her waist as she stood looking out across the scene.

'Thank you,' she said as his cheek touched hers, she placed her palm over his clasped fingers and her other hand on the side of his face.

'We wanted to make our last night together special,' said Cassian.

'I don't want this to be our last night.'

Cassian frowned. 'I mean of the holiday.'

'I know but I want this every night.'

'This took quite a lot of effort,' he laughed. 'Not sure we could manage this every day.'

'No, I mean I want us all to be together, every night. Even if we're just sat in front of the TV in our pyjamas, massaging Amy's feet.'

Cassian smiled kindly. 'Maybe one day.'

Emilia turned around and pressed her head against his chest as he wrapped his arms around her.

'Thank you,' she said. As they embraced, she looked sideways and saw Mark and Amy swaying back and forth in the candlelight and she felt love. It was a love that came from within and spread out all the way to her extremities, and it felt wonderful.

'We should eat,' said Mark after a while. 'Otherwise our Herculean efforts will have gone to waste.'

'Herculean?' said Amy, raising her eyebrows as she looked up at him

'Have you seen the food?'

Mark took Amy's hand and started to lead her over toward

the table. Cassian, taking his cue, did the same. Emilia looped her arm through his as they walked in procession through the corridor of candle light.

The table was laden with the most incredible selection of food. It seemed to be overflowing with bowls and plates and dips and bread.

Mark pulled out a chair for his wife, inviting her to sit as Cassian did the same for Emilia. Then as he settled down, Mark collected a bottle of Champagne from the end of the table and popped the cork making both girls scream and laugh.

Like a well practiced waiter, he made his way around them, pouring out the bottle into each of the little flutes they had carefully and meticulously arranged on the clean white cloth draped across the wooden table.

Emilia had noticed that the cutlery, the serving bowls, the spoons and the plates were all perfectly positioned. She wondered whether if she were to take the time to measure the relative distances between each item, she would find less than a millimetre disparity across the board. Mark was very particular and very precise.

As he sat down he raised his glass and smiled, looking to each of them in turn.

'To us,' he said.

They clinked glasses and took a little sip each, all except for Amy who drank her whole flute in one go and burst into laughter.

'Whoops,' she giggled as the bubbles hit her nose, her eyes watering as she laughed.

'If we ignore my wife's readily apparent drinking problem for a moment, we have prepared a comprehensive selection of continental dishes this evening for you to choose from.'

'You're allowed to mix and match, you don't have to stick to one cultural cuisine,' interjected Cassian.

'Quite right,' said Mark nodding. 'We have Spanish Tapas, Mediterranean Seafood, a traditional French casserole, and some coq au vin. Moules, a selection of cold meats from Switzerland and bread and cheese from all over Europe.'

He gestured to each dish as he made his way around the table.

'Oh my goodness, I love moules,' said Amy, her eyes widening.

'I even got you a bib,' laughed Mark, handing her a large silk napkin.

'This is why I love you,' she said giggling as she took it.

'This must have taken you all day,' said Emilia as Cassian poured both her and Amy a glass of red wine each.

'Since you left this morning,' said Mark. 'With a short break to double team Celeste. She popped back round for lunch.'

'I'm not even sure if you're joking after this morning, Mark.'

'What if we hadn't gone out?' said Emilia, diverting the conversation.

'We had a contingency plan.'

'But how could you have known we were going to go shopping?'

'We've been dropping hints all week,' laughed Cassian. 'Little nudges, subtle suggestions.'

'Oh my goodness,' laughed Amy. 'Are we that easy to manipulate? I'm going to have to pay more attention. That's crafty.'

'The most convincing ideas are the ones you come up with yourself,' shrugged Mark.

Amy tied off her napkin around her neck as Mark served a large ladle full of moules into a bowl for her. As she began to crack open the first one, Emilia served herself a portion of coq au vin and picked up her knife and fork.

'This is incredible,' said Emilia as she tasted it. 'Where did you learn to cook like this?'

'Paris,' said Mark. 'I lived in the city for three years, studied at the Pantheon-Sorbonne.'

'What did you study?'

'Art History.'

Emilia raised her eyebrows. 'I was not expecting that.'

Mark shrugged. 'It's a passion of mine. That's part of what kept Amy and I together.'

'That and his huge cock.'

Emilia burst into shocked laughter, trying her best not to spray her mouthful of red wine and chicken all over her plate.

'I'm not joking, seriously it's as thick as a log. The first time we had anal sex I thought my bum hole would never recover.'

'Oh my goodness,' laughed Emilia, wiping tears away from her eyes and almost choking on her food. 'You are *terrible*, Amy.'

'Cheap date. One drink and I'm all yours, and yours, and yours,' she shot finger pistols at each of them in turn, winking as she blew them away, then picking up a squishy muscle on her fork. 'Em, do you want a moule?'

She shook her head politely and turned back to Mark as he continued.

'In answer to your question, Emilia,' said Mark with a sly grin on his face. 'I took a job in the kitchens of a restaurant in the eighth arrondissement, on Avenue Montaigne.'

'You were a chef?'

'I was a Chef de Partie, or specifically a Chef de Tournant, so I worked in different parts of the kitchen each night, filling in.'

'He loves filling in different parts,' giggled Amy, chewing on another moule. As she bit down on it, it popped in her mouth and squirted out, narrowly missing Emilia. 'Oops, little squirt.'

Amy's eyes met Emilia's and immediately she began to laugh, as her friend shook her head.

'No, no, don't you dare.'

'Did she tell you?' said Amy, looking pointedly at Cassian.

'Tell me what?'

'Amy, *no*,' Emilia waved her hands, then hid her face in shame.

'About last night?'

'Amy!'

'She squirted.'

'I hate you.'

'Or peed herself, I'm still not quite sure which.'

'You are the *worst*.'

Cassian laughed and looked at Mark, shaking his head.

'Like I said earlier, mate,' nodded Mark. 'We're going to have to up our game.'

'Sounds like it.'

Emilia was still covering her face in shame.

'I'm sorry,' said Amy as Emilia felt her girlfriend's hand slide over her thigh. 'We have to set the bar higher for them somehow though. You have to understand the male psyche. Now all they're going to be thinking about is how they can make you squirt too.'

'Oh my goodness, you don't have to,' said Emilia looking up at the two men before hiding again.

'You're going to have the best night ever,' she turned back round, grinning. 'Oh and guys, Emilia made me squirt too.'

She dropped another empty moule shell back into the bowl as she finished her sentence, raising her eyebrows, cocking her head and leaving her hand dangling in the air.

'Challenge accepted,' said Mark.

Amy sat back in her chair, smiling then she reached out for

Emilia, prying her fingers away and uncovering her face.

'Hey in there, there's no need to be embarrassed, I loved it.'

Emilia nodded, blushing and smiling. She licked her lips as Amy squeezed her hand and leaned forward. She felt nervous. All this food and the amount of effort the boys had gone to. The bed, the candles, the dresses, their secret lingerie. It was incredible, and somehow intimidating at the same time. Everything was perfect and yet she was petrified.

'Good grief boys, Champagne and moules,' said Amy suddenly, interrupting her train of thought and winking at her subtly. 'Are you trying to get us into bed or something?'

Mark smiled and reached for another olive, smiling as he popped it into his mouth.

'As a matter of fact, yes we are.'

Amy laughed and bit her lip and then leaned into Emilia to whisper, taking hold of her hand.

'Stop worrying, I'll look after you. I always will.'

*

The stars shone brightly above as the two men stood up and held out their hands, inviting their wives to stand and join them. Their dinner finished, their plates empty, their glasses dry.

Emilia rose first, nervously yet gracefully taking Cassian's hand and swinging her legs around and off the little wooden chair.

Amy smiled, dabbing her lips as Mark bowed to her and grinned.

'This is so beautiful,' she said as he led her across the grass, through the hundreds of candles marking their path as they followed Cassian and Emilia toward the bed.

Emilia was shaking as she stood next her husband, turning to see Amy's smiling face as Mark took her around to the other side, his arm tucked tightly round her waist. Together, the two men parted the makeshift surround and opened their arms high to allow the girls to enter their little romantic retreat.

Amy ducked down and stepped through, turning as Mark followed and taking hold of his face in her palms, pulling him forward and falling backwards onto the bed as they kissed.

Emilia giggled as they rolled around together, kissing and running their arms over each other. She watched with excitement as Amy began to pull at Mark's dinner jacket, untying his bow tie with both hands and then falling back onto the bed, laughing playfully.

She was so beautiful that it made her heart ache. She reached out for her now, her fingers splayed wide as she lay flat, Mark kneeling between her thighs, trying to shake his jacket off onto the grass behind him. His shirt was partially unbuttoned and his bow tie was slung loosely around his neck.

'Come help us,' said Amy, laughing. 'We need you.'

Emilia smiled and looked to Cassian who nodded his approval. Slowly she walked around behind Mark, reaching out and pulling his jacket away from his arms and then kissing him softly as he turned to look up at her.

She ran her hand up his chest, across the inside opening of his shirt and as she reached his neckline she took hold of his loose bow tie and wrapped it between her fingers.

As she was holding the soft silk material against her skin an idea came to her, she smiled and flashed her eyes at Cassian as it ran through her mind like a dirty reel at an old cinema. She stifled a giggle and beckoned for her husband to come closer.

He walked over as the other two watched with curiosity and she ran her hands up his chest, feeling the definition of his abs hidden beneath the soft material of his shirt.

Then in one swift and sudden motion, she pulled the end of his bow tie and unravelled it, sliding it away from around his neck until it came off entirely.

Holding both strips of silk in her hands she turned and looked at Amy, whose eyes widened. She sat up quickly, a look of excitement on her face as Emilia began to slowly unwind both ties.

'Take off her dress,' she said quietly, not breaking eye contact with her as the men both grinned.

They knelt forward on the bed, Cassian pulling her upright as he shuffled around behind her, Mark raising her arms up as she knelt between them. Then Cassian rolled her dress up around her thighs, sliding it softly over her skin, pushing it up as she kissed her husband, slowly revealing the secret red lingerie beneath.

She pulled away from Mark's lips as Cassian now pulled the dress up and over her face and then she was free of it, and she wrapped her arms around her handsome husband and kissed him hard as Cassian sandwiched her between them, sliding his hand down her back and over her bottom, squeezing it tight against the intricate lace.

'Lay her back,' said Emilia as she walked around the side of the bed, circling them slowly. 'Hold out her arms.'

Amy breathed in and out sharply and unevenly with excitement as her two men took control of her body from her, laying her back and taking one arm each as Emilia walked slowly round the back of the headboard.

She licked her lips as she took Amy's hand in her own, running her index finger softly around her palm in a little circle before slipping Cassian's soft silk bow around her wrist until it was firm and tight.

Amy watched with rising excitement as Mark ran his free hand up her inner thigh, making her squirm and wriggle with delight against their firm grip.

With a slow and commanding confidence, Emilia tied the remaining tie to the bed frame in a quick release bow, leaving Amy able to free herself, but otherwise immobilised.

As she tightened the little knot, she leaned down and kissed her, Amy rising up to meet her lips urgently, then she moved over to the other side and relieved Cassian, taking hold of her girlfriend's little wrists and tying her other hand in place.

'Oh *fuck*,' whispered Amy, barely able to contain herself, writhing against her soft restraints and biting her lips. She looked up at Emilia, standing above her head and smiling mischievously and then she looked down at their husbands as they began to undress.

She had never felt more electrified and erotic, her whole body felt like it was tingling in anticipation of their touch. Taking away her control had made her feel so alive, and yet utterly vulnerable. She was entirely at their mercy.

It was like the annual house of horror tour she loved so much. She was scared, intensely turned on, but completely safe.

Amy sensed movement behind her - a faint swish of satin - then Emilia's hands came down either side of her face, placing her black silk belt softly over Amy's eyes.

'Yes,' she whispered. '*Yes,*' as Emilia tied the makeshift blindfold off behind her head, her fingers teasing the back of her neck, unleashing goosebumps and making her buck and twist.

Now she was completely helpless, she couldn't see and she couldn't touch. All she could do was wait and with every passing second her arousal and anticipation built. She could feel how wet she was as she moved and it only served to make her feel more desperate for their touch.

Emilia stood smiling at the two men kneeling on the bed either side of their sweet little red haired goddess. They were both looking to her now, waiting for their next instruction. The power was intoxicating. She walked around the side of the bed frame and their eyes followed her until she stood at the end and beckoned them forward.

Taking their cue they both stood up, standing either side of her. She turned towards Cassian and pressed her lips against his, sliding her hand up against his throbbing cock through the thin material of his trousers. As she stroked him, she reached back and found Mark's member easily, pushing hard against her as he kissed her neck and ran his hands around her hips.

As they touched, she glanced down at Amy, tied to the bed, writhing as she waited. She didn't want to keep her waiting long, but a little longer wouldn't hurt.

Mark's fingers found the zip of her dress and hurriedly undid it as Cassian helped slide it off over her shoulders. As the two men worked, she undid their belts, turning as she slipped Cassian's away and kissing Mark hard as she undid his.

Cassian's cock pushed against her ass as Mark squeezed her forward and together they moved as one, like a wave. Then she held up her hand and placed a single finger against her lips. The two men stood back, naked and glistening in the moonlight as they admired her and Amy, looking back and forth at their matching lingerie, noticing the lack of crotch material and grinning at the beauty and wonder before them.

Slowly, commanding the same power she held before, she looked across at her girlfriend and smiled.

Amy felt a weight press down on the bed just beneath her legs and she drew them together instinctively, twisting in her restraints as she giggled and licked her lips. Her skin felt like it was prickling and ultra sensitive, waiting for the tiniest and most delicate touch of skin on skin.

Slowly she parted herself once more, forcing her thighs

apart, fighting her instincts, and biting down on her lower lip as she arched her back, writhing and desperate.

'Oh fuck, *touch me*, someone touch me,' she whispered.

She felt the person move again, she couldn't tell if it was Mark or Cassian, or perhaps it was Emilia? She didn't know what to expect. They were all silent. She listened to see if she could hear breathing or rustling, but there was nothing.

She then felt the most delicate contact against her warmth and her whole body surged.

One of her two men thrust inside her, but she couldn't tell who. She thought it could be Mark for a moment, but as whoever it was kept going they seemed to go deeper than he ever had before and she wondered if it was Cassian.

He felt thicker than usual though, stretching her like Mark always did. They thrust again and she cried out in pleasure and then she moaned as someone's mouth closed over her nipple. She tried to reach down and grab their head, to feel their hair so she would know who it was, but her restraints held her back. Their lips felt soft like Emilia's and for a moment she felt something course like stubble and she sensed it could be Cassian, which made her think that Mark was actually inside her.

Her body felt like a chaotic firework display, exploding at each touch and each pulse. Then Emilia's soft lips pressed against her own and she saw stars.

She came hard and suddenly, moaning into her girlfriend's mouth. Her whole body twitched and quivered, her legs writhing as she pulled against the silk ribbons, rattling the headboard as the orgasm rushed through her.

The man inside her slowed down as she squeezed him, waiting patiently as she came down, her movements slowing and her body relaxing. Then as she lay there, catching her breath, they pulled out.

She felt the weight leave the bed, bouncing softly as they

swapped positions. Suddenly Emilia was pulling her wrists together and one of the two men was rolling her onto her front and sliding her legs apart so she was laying flat.

Then nothing.

She let out a deep heaving sigh, uneven and shallow as she waited with breathless anticipation.

Then she felt warmth against her bottom and she rose up off the mattress, feeling hands pushing her back down and parting her.

Emilia's hands.

She turned her head, snapping backwards in a futile effort to see, but the blindfold was sealed tight, and all she was could see was darkness and drifting white specks like stars in the night sky.

Emilia held her tight, one sweet little bum cheek in each palm and then Amy shook as she sensed the warmth of her face as it drew closer.

Her hot breath.

Her mouth.

Her tongue.

There.

She moaned out loud as she felt the tip press against her forbidden hole, making her slick and wet as the soft lips of her girlfriend slipped back and forth against her button. Then a moment later she felt a lithe finger slide inside her pussy, filling her up and pleasuring her gently as she continued to lap.

It was as though she was preparing her, lapping and making her slick. Making her as wet as possible before...

Emilia pulled away.

'Oh *fuck*,' cried Amy, writhing and moaning now, begging. 'Someone fuck me, please.'

She knelt up on all fours and parted herself, wiggling back and forth, desperate to be penetrated. Then strong hands pulled her back down until she was flat again.

Then he was on top of her, and again she didn't know who, and Emilia was next to her face.

'Can you tell who it is?' she whispered. Amy shook her head from side to side.

'How about now?'

The man's cock pressed hard against her tight little opening, one hand against her hip, the other on her back, holding her down and in her place.

He was struggling against her, she was tighter than usual, not as slick as she would be with lube, and she felt whoever it was surge as they pushed and pushed.

'Keep going,' she moaned, willing them to push harder as she held firm, pushing back, trying to relax.

Then suddenly she felt that now familiar sensation of herself opening up like a flower, stretching out and then the satisfying pop as their cock slid past her dark opening and up, deep inside her.

It felt like Mark, but she wasn't sure. They felt thick like him, but they also felt longer somehow, harder and more ridged.

The sensations were more intense than ever before, more filling and more powerful. She held on tight to Emilia's hand as she moaned

He pushed all the way into her now as she cried and shook, gripping hold of the metal frame with her free hand as she writhed, a part of her desperate to know who was fucking her, and another naughtier part of her excited that she didn't.

'Spank me,' she begged and a second later she felt the sting of a man's palm against her backside.

'Again,' this one stung even more and she yelped in pleasure as the pain seared through her skin making her eyes well up with tears behind her silk blindfold.

'Make me cum again,' she begged as he continued to thrust, then a second later she felt fingers against her clit. Emilia's fingers. She could tell them apart so easily, hers were soft and small, delicate and gentle in contrast to the thick hands of the men.

She cried out in pleasure as the intensity of the combined sensations crashed through her like lightning forking through the night sky. Now someone was near her face, stroking her lips with their thumb. She darted her mouth forward and sucked on it, then pulled away and looked up.

A moment later and to her surprise, she felt their cock sliding against her tongue.

Thick and wet and hard, it slid through her opening, filling her mouth completely as she took them in.

The sensation was too much.

She could feel them pulsing gently and for a moment she thought it tasted like Mark, salty and sweet as she swallowed his pre-cum. Then a hand stroked her hair and he thrust forward gently into her throat as she opened wide.

She had one man in her ass and the other in her mouth as her girlfriend's fingers stimulated her clit. She wanted them both to explode inside her, to fill her with their seed as Emilia took care of her pussy.

As he slid back out she begged.

'Cum inside me, both of you, please.'

They slid back in deeper this time and she held back tears of pleasure as her man's cock filled her mouth, sliding back and forth as she helped, pushing him deeper as she leaned forward.

Her ass felt full, her throat felt full and for a brief fleeting moment she wished that Emilia could be inside her too.

Then the man in front of her seemed to tighten, his cock bulging and twisting in her mouth. Then he buckled and came, shooting rope after rope of warmth onto her tongue.

The sticky sweet and salty taste overwhelmed her senses as her other man bucked and thrust and came in her ass.

And over the edge she went.

Her whole body tingled as she saw stars. It felt as though she was floating away as she collapsed down onto the bed, the weight of the man on top of her pushing all of the wind out of her.

Then he rolled off and she lay still, breathing and shuddering with happiness.

'*That was incredible*,' she whispered. '*Oh my goodness, oh fuck.*'

'You okay?' said Emilia, close to her ear as she slid the blindfold away.

She looked up to find Cassian smiling at her, and then she turned to see Mark behind her and she laughed, shaking her head.

'I had no idea,' she breathed. 'No idea. That was amazing.'

She collapsed back onto the pillow and closed her eyes, her body slowly recovering as Emilia stroked her hair. She felt her two men lay down beside them, one laying one way, one laying the other.

After a little while, Emilia whispered in her ear. 'Why don't we give them a little show?' she said, undoing her restraints and pulling her up, kissing her lips as she did so and tasting Cassian's seed there.

'I'd like that,' said Amy, grinning and embracing her. 'I want to make you squirt again.'

Emilia nodded enthusiastically and Amy kissed her hard as the two men sat back and watched.

Amy pressed the flat of her palm against Emilia's chest and pushed her back down onto the bed, pinning her legs down and sliding her lingerie off, revealing her breasts and her flat stomach, then her pussy and her ass. She bundle it up tight and threw it towards her husband who caught them and laughed.

Before Emilia could even react, Amy's fingers were sliding inside her soaking wet parting and curling upwards.

Cassian sat up and grinned as his wife's head shot backwards, listening to her moan and hearing how wet she was as her girlfriend's fingers slipped in and out.

Amy worked fast and Emilia's hand's shot out and gathered up the duvet as she gripped it tight, her eyes screwed closed and her mouth open wide as she arched her back.

'Oh my *fuck,*' she cried as Amy's smooth, agile and rigid fingers pounded up against her g-spot, her pussy slick with arousal as she bounced her hips up and down.

Mark sat up as Amy lay down on her front, pushing Emilia's thighs apart as she pressed her tongue against her lips and began to lick her up and down, swirling around her clit with such intensity and passion that she began to shake.

Emilia could feel it again, that strange sensation, that pressure building up inside of her, looking for a way out as Amy's fingers coaxed it along. As though each pulse of her fingers was pumping her and making her fuller and fuller.

She opened her eyes and saw both Cassian and Mark staring wide eyed at her, looking down between her legs where Amy was and she felt strangely self-conscious.

She went bright red and closed her eyes again, feeling ashamed and aroused at the same time, but it was too late to stop. She had passed the point of no return, and she didn't want to anyway.

Not a chance.

She let it build for longer this time, let the crescendo heighten, the wave grow and grow and then as Amy's fingers pushed harder and harder, she let go.

And relaxed.

It was like her whole body was sinking into the bed, as

though it was made of warm jelly, cocooning and cushioning her slowly.

She felt that same warmth spreading out from inside and she heard Amy gasp and laugh and the sound of a gentle gush of fluid.

'Oh,' said Cassian in the distance as he looked on, wide eyed.

Mark made a noise too, one of astonishment and surprise and she stifled a giggle as she lay there, panting and melting.

After what seemed like a dreamy, blurry age, she opened her eyes and looked up into the night sky.

She found that Amy had crawled up next to her, tucked over her arm, her head nestled in her shoulder.

Had she passed out? How long had she been gone?

'Just a couple of minutes,' said Amy, laughing.

'How did you know I was thinking that?'

'Educated guess and the look on your face.'

She glanced down and saw that Mark was playing with himself and then she looked across at Cassian and saw that he too was grinning and rock hard.

She rolled sideways and kissed Amy, pulling her arm free. 'Do you trust me?' she said, looking into her girlfriend's eyes.

'Yes,' she replied, confused.

'Lay on your side,' she said, moving away and smiling.

Emilia wriggled up the bed until she was above Amy, her legs either side of her and her hands close enough to touch her face.

She looked at Mark first and beckoned to him to lay down, facing his wife and then she indicated to Cassian to lay down behind her, mirroring Mark.

The two men did so, and as Amy realised what was happening she looked up at Emilia, apprehension in her eyes.

'I don't know if I can do this,' she said, taking a deep shuddering breath.

'Yes you can,' came the reply. 'I know you can, just take it slow.'

Amy felt nervous as Mark cradled her in his arms, looking deep into her eyes as he smiled and reassured her.

They felt so big all of a sudden.

Her small frame was dwarfed by the two men as they lay either side of her.

Emilia stroked her hair as she sensed Cassian lining himself up.

'It's okay, just relax,' said Mark.

She bit her lip and nodded, trying not to clench as Cassian's thick member slid between her cheeks. She reached out for Emilia, and held her hand tight as she felt his head sliding against her slick little hole.

He paused and waited.

Emilia leaned down and kissed her forehead, then Amy nodded at her husband. 'You first.'

He smiled and stroked her cheek, then he pushed himself inside as her mouth opened wide and her eyes closed. When he was all the way in she took another shuddering breath and then nodded.

Cassian's hands gripped her hips and Mark's thigh's held her in place. She closed her eyes again, preparing herself, and then she took a moment, steadying herself. 'Ok, I'm ready.'

Cassian's cock throbbed as he gently pushed into her. He angled his hips up as she flowered, opening up slowly, more easily than before as he kept pushing, then suddenly he was in.

She shook as the sensation swept through her, gripping Emilia's hand tight and tensing her muscles as both men held her between them.

She quivered and moaned, tingling as they stayed still, not daring to even breath. Letting her get used to the sensation. As she calmed down, Cassian pushed a little further, stretching her until he couldn't push anymore.

Her whole body pulsed as they throbbed within, not daring to move any more until she gave her permission.

She looked up at Emilia, barely able to open her eyes and she found that she was smiling back at her and stroking her hair with an expression of love and compassion.

'Are you okay?' she whispered.

Amy nodded and looked down.

Mark's eyes flashed at her and she smiled at him and then nodded at them all.

'I'm ready,' she said, taking one last deep breath and biting down on her lip.

Mark thrust first, making her arch her head back as his thick cock slid out of her and then she moaned quietly as it slid back in. Then Cassian pulled out steadily and she bucked forward, pressing her face into her husband shoulder as he slid back in.

It felt incredible.

As though her whole life she hadn't been aware that she wasn't whole and now, with both of them inside her, she was.

The men thrust again, Cassian moaning into her neck as her tight ass swallowed his length. She cried out softly at the sound of his voice, still holding her girlfriend's hand as Mark cradled her cheeks, looking deep into her eyes as the two men began to get into a rhythm.

'You're doing great,' he said quietly and she nodded and smiled with pride.

'It feels so tight,' she whispered, her body quivering as she spoke, the sensation of both of her men inside her at the same time was overwhelming. She felt connected to them all, their skin and their touch making her feel warm and loved as their bodies pleasured her and used her.

She could sense them both quickening now, powering into her from either side as they held her tighter and tighter, working in unison; an unspoken communication between them.

Emilia looked at the three of them together, squeezed up as one, connected by their flesh and their love as she stroked Amy's hair and squeezed her fingers.

Then Mark began to moan and at the sound of his voice and his fastening pace, she moaned too, swiftly followed by Cassian.

Her mind went blank as they thrust with wild abandon into her, her whole body shuddering and quivering with wild lust as fireworks exploded behind her eyes.

She had never felt more desired and safe in her life as her two men ravished her, holding her and stroking her and thrusting and squeezing.

And then they came.

Both of them at once, pulsing and pumping as they exploded, filling her with their seed until she felt like she was going to burst.

And then to her surprise, she came again.

Mark felt it first, her body shaking hard as she squirted onto him, his cock warm and wet as her body flushed and shuddered. Then Cassian felt it too as the glistening fluid pooled on the bed.

Amy cried out in pleasure, her moan echoing into the night sky, her whole body straining and throbbing as they held her steady, rocking back and forth and then finally, slowly and eventually, going limp.

The two men carefully slipped out of her and lay still, shaking and cuddling, not caring where their arms lay, just blissful and happy and satiated.

Emilia stroked their hair as they slept, their bodies entwined together, peaceful in their exhausted slumber. After a while, she leaned down and kissed Amy's cheek and whispered to her.

'I love you.'

Then she kissed Mark and ran her fingers through his hair.

'And I love you too.'

Then she turned to Cassian who stirred and looked up, just barely opening his eyes.

She thought about Alice for a moment and everything that had happened since the start of this week, and then she reached down and cradled his face in her hands and kissed him long and hard.

'And I love *you*.'

Gradually the three of them stirred and moved as Emilia watched.

She wasn't sure if she was imagining it, but it seemed as though the sky was becoming lighter now.

She had no idea what time it was or how long they had been making love for. Or even if she herself had fallen asleep.

But something had woken them, perhaps some mutual feeling, perhaps a shared desire. She didn't know, but she smiled as they each opened their eyes and looked up at her.

Amy wiped her eyes and grinned as she remembered where she was and what she had been doing, and then she laughed.

'Oh my goodness, that was amazing. It's *so* your turn Em.'

Emilia laughed, dismissively but then she stopped as she saw Mark and Cassian's faces as they began to move.

Amy looked at her husband and whispered. 'Lay back, and don't move.'

She reached up and took her girlfriend's hand and pulled her over to her husband, turning her around so she was facing down toward his legs.

Emilia straddled him, hovering her bottom over his slick cock, giggling as it poked her cheeks. She moved awkwardly backwards, her palms flat on the duvet either side of him as he held her waist and supported her like a crab. Amy leaned forward, and took his cock in her hands, holding it straight up as Emilia smiled.

'Are you ready?' asked Amy, looking up at her.

She shook her head and laughed.

Mark stayed firm as she lowered herself, Amy guiding his head, stroking it gently between her fingers.

She felt him against her, that familiar pressure, that sensation of *taboo*. It was electrifying and her whole body shuddered as she closed her eyes.

She lowered herself, pressing down onto him and then gasped as he slipped straight in.

Her eyes popped open as she dropped down, faster than she'd anticipated and his shaft disappeared inside of her ass completely.

Pleasure burst through her, a delayed reaction as that familiar deep and powerful throbbing sensation overcame her senses.

She steadied herself and he held her tight as Amy moved her hand away, briefly sliding her fingers across her soaking wet lips as she withdrew.

'Ok,' she breathed toward Cassian, who knelt upright on the bed beside Amy.

Now she leaned back, angling herself up to allow her husband to enter her too.

Amy reached out again as he shuffled forward, holding him between her finger and thumb as he pulsed.

She felt him pressing on her lips, and Amy sliding him up and down against her as Mark's cock grew inside her ass. Then Cassian took hold of her knees and pushed.

Her head fell back as she moaned, her long hair falling across Mark's face as the two men thrust. Another gasp escaped her lips as the sensation overwhelmed her. They pushed into her at the same time, throbbing and thick, stretching her as they strained.

Her whole body shook as her men made loved to her.

'*Yes*,' she cried as Mark thrust upwards from the bed, his thick girth sliding so easily in and out of her tight little hole as Cassian's solid member fucked her warmth.

She sensed Amy kneeling up beside her, then felt her breath on her cheek and her lips on her neck, then she gasped as her girlfriend's fingers slipped over her clit.

'Oh *fuck*,' she moaned as Amy began to circle her faster and faster, closing her lips over her ultra-sensitive nipples. She writhed but her girl held on, circling her with her tongue as her finger flicked up and down steadily inside her hood.

Emilia was overwhelmed with pleasure, and she began to wail.

It came as one long and passionate cry, loud and sweet as her body succumbed to the ecstasy of it all.

She felt like a wave on the ocean, crashing and tumbling inexorably toward the shore, cresting and falling and collapsing and rolling. It was like nothing she had ever experienced, at once fuzzy and dull and yet focused, sharp and intense, as though she was drifting in and out of consciousness.

'I love you all,' she moaned, her hands shaking and then collapsing down onto Mark, not able to hold herself up any longer as he cradled her lithe body.

She rolled over, both of them sliding out of her and then she grabbed hold of his cock and slipped it between her legs again, enveloping him inside her warmth and beckoning to Cassian to fuck her ass as she began to slide up and down on Mark.

Amy found her lips and Emilia found her pussy and the two of them held each other and touched each other as Cassian slid back inside his wife, where moments ago Mark had been.

'Fuck me,' she said to them. 'Fuck me, *hard*.'

Cassian thrust into her and Mark did the same, holding her thighs as his friend gripped her waist and the three of them pounded each other, moaning louder and louder as they got closer and closer.

Emilia reached out for Amy, pulling her head and she grinned and straddled Mark's face, lowering her wet pussy down onto his lips. His tongue flicked against her as she kissed Emilia and caressed her breast and lowered her fingers back down between her legs.

'*Harder*,' she gasped.

They obliged as she closed her eyes and started to shake.

It was going to happen again.

She could feel it, just like before when Amy's fingers were deep inside her, except this time it was her men. That pressure was building up, down there, inside her somewhere, indefinable and indescribable.

Intense and powerful and inevitable.

Then the warmth.

It started in her pussy and it spread out quickly around her waist and her tummy and her ass and her thighs.

Her abs tightened until it was like a knot as she tried to hold it back and let it build.

Mark came first, exploding into her, his thick cock groaning as her pussy clenched and squeezed him, then Cassian groaned and spilled his seed in her ass, leaning over her back and moaning into her ear as she thrust and shook.

Then she relaxed and let herself gush.

Amy drew breath as she felt it wash across her fingers and down Mark's abdomen, pooling in his belly button as she laughed and cried out in pleasure and excitement.

Then to her surprise it came again, another shudder and another wave of pleasure washing out of her.

'Oh my,' said Amy, holding her hand up to her mouth.

One more time, she writhed backwards, waves crashing

through her, and then she shuddered and went limp, falling into Amy's arms as orgasmic aftershocks wracked her body.

She felt Cassian slide out of her, and then Mark too and then she and Amy were laying together on the bed, arms wrapped around each other's naked bodies, their husbands either side of them, holding them, guarding them, keeping them safe.

Loving them.

Blissful and peaceful.

It had been the perfect ending to the perfect night... to the perfect vacation.

Emilia knew for certain now what she wanted, she knew it deep in her heart.

She knew it as she knew the sky was blue and the grass was green.

Around her the world was brightening, the sun rising on a new day. A new beginning, filled with possibility and love and wonder.

This may be the final day of their holiday together, but to her it felt like the start of a new chapter. Something fresh and exciting.

A seed of such beauty and wonder that it felt like it was dazzling her mind's eye.

A seed that would grow inside her, and inside Amy, that they would love.

That they would *all* love.

She looked up into the fading stars of the night sky above as dawn began to break, and she smiled as she fell asleep.

*

EPILOGUE

Emilia woke up to the sound of bird song and bright, warm sunshine.

Amy was fast asleep on her, and Cassian and Mark's arms were wrapped over them both. Mark's hand lay on her hip, and Cassian's on Amy's.

They'd laid like this before, together as one.

That first morning at the Spa, then again almost a week later after the dinner party at their house. It felt right.

They weren't two couples anymore.

It felt like more than that now. They were all together, even Mark and Cassian had become closer. They were more like brothers than friends.

She looked up into the blue sky above them, feeling the warm sun against her skin, as though it was charging her, making her feel alive.

And in love.

She loved them all.

There was no pretending, there was no being coy or shy about it. She had fallen in love, and she hoped dearly that they all loved her back.

Amy began to stir, her eyes fluttering open and then squinting in the brightness. Her red hair radiant in the morning light, stark against her pale skin.

Emilia kissed her and she smiled.

'I bet my breath smells awful,' she whispered, covering her mouth as Emilia shook her head, kissing her again.

At the sound of their voices, the two men began to wake, Cassian rolling away and stretching as Mark squeezed Emilia's bottom in his ample hands.

She giggled and closed her fingers over his, keeping them there and enjoying the warmth of his touch as he stroked her and kissed his wife's head. He took a deep breath and yawned as Amy yelped, jumping forward.

'Bloody hell, Mark you're insatiable,' she raised her leg to reveal his rock hard cock between her thighs.

'Can't help it,' he yawned, opening his eyes. 'Waking up in bed with two beautiful women.'

Emilia reached out behind her, searching, and laughed as she found that Cassian was also erect.

'You too?'

She felt him shrug.

'Morning glory,' he rolled back into her and pressed it against her thigh. 'Horniest time of the day for a man.'

'Good grief, you'd think you two would need some rest after last night.'

Emilia continued to play with him, rolling him back and forth between her fingers as she smiled.

It was perfect.

For now.

'Home today,' said Amy, stroking Emilia's naked tummy. She looked up at her, smiling sadly.

'Can't we stay for longer?'

Mark shook his head and stretched. 'Sorry, as much as I'd love to, I've got to be back at work tomorrow.'

'Yeah, me too,' said Cassian.

'Let's move in together then,' said Emilia suddenly.

The other three fell silent.

'I'm serious.'

Amy frowned, rolling onto her front as Mark sat up on his elbows.

'Em,' said Amy, but Emilia interrupted her before she could say anything else.

'*No*,' she said. 'I want this, *every* day. I want to wake up with all of you. I want you to be my family. I don't want to be two couples anymore, I want us to be together. I want us to move *in* together, to start a family together.'

Cassian sat up and Mark turned to look at her too, glancing between the two girls.

Amy blinked at her and then smiled carefully, shaking her head and frowning in disbelief at what she was hearing. 'Really?'

Emilia nodded.

'You want to start a family with us?' she said, quietly.

'All of us,' she said, with tears in her eyes. 'Yes.'

Each of them stayed silent as more tears began to roll down Emilia's cheek. As it went on, she began to feel more and more silly.

Then Amy leapt forward and embraced her, holding her tight as the two of them began to cry.

'Yes,' she said quietly.

Mark began to laugh.

'Yes,' she said again, louder as she kissed Emilia's tears.

Cassian shook his head and made eyes at Mark as the two of them started to shake their heads and laugh.

'Boys? What do you think? Cass?' said Amy, looking at

him first.

'I've been ready to be a dad for years,' he laughed, tears welling up in his own eyes as he nodded.

She turned to Mark.

'Mark? Are you ready to put a baby in us?' she giggled, raising her eyebrows.

He took a deep breath and ran his hands through his short hair, frowning.

'I think we need to be sensible and think about this, and not rush into anything...'

The two girl's held their breath, waiting for him to continue but he stayed silent.

'That means yes,' Amy whispered to Emilia, kissing her cheeks again as Mark laughed.

'It means *maybe*,' he said.

'Maybe, is good enough for me,' said Emilia, tears streaming down her face now. 'I'm sorry,' she laughed as they kissed and kissed, holding each other tight.

Amy pulled back and gasped in excitement. 'If we get pregnant at the same time, we can do all the mummy stuff together when the babies are born.'

Emilia grinned, her eyes wide.

'We can go to baby groups, and buy clothes together, *oh my goodness*.'

'And we can compare bump sizes, I bet you'll be tiny and I'll be huge.'

Mark shook his head and lay back down on the bed, groaning as Cassian laughed.

'There's so many ways this can go wrong,' he laughed as he laid back.

'The boys can wear matching carriers,' said Emilia excitedly as Amy's eyes widened at the image.

'And we can wear matching maternity outfits,' she said, bouncing up and down on the bed.

'You know you won't ovulate at the same time,' groaned Mark.

'*Yet*,' said Amy, grabbing his hand and pulling him up.

She looked at him, pleading for his approval as he shook his head. For a long time he stared back, smiling, looking between his wife, Emilia and Cassian.

Eventually he looked down and grinned.

'Fine,' he took a deep and long breath. 'When we get home, we can start looking at houses.'

Emilia and Amy screamed and then jumped on him, wrestling him down onto the bed, showering him in kisses as he curled his arms around them both.

'What about me?' laughed Cassian. 'I was up for this from the star-.'

Before he could finish his sentence, Amy had leapt onto him, rolling him backwards and straddling him, pinning his arms back as Emilia did the same to Mark.

'I still think we need a little practice though,' she said, looking into Cassian's eyes and arching up as she glanced sideways at Emilia. 'Don't you think, Em?

'Definitely,' she said as she rolled her warmth against Mark's thick morning wood.

'We're going to miss our plane,' warned Mark as Emilia took hold of him in between her slender fingers and knelt up. She shrugged as Amy moaned beside her, Cassian sliding deep inside her girlfriend as they reached out for each other's hands.

As they started to make love, the two girls looked across, reached out, and squeezed each other's fingers.

A whole new chapter of their lives was about to begin.

A whole new *life*.

Hopefully more than one.

Emilia stroked her belly softly as Mark made love to her.

Amy closed her eyes and grinned.

And together, they all smiled.

THE END

The adventures of Emilia, Cassian, Amy and Mark are continued in **Stay With Us: An Urban Foursome Swingers Ménage**

Keep reading for a sample chapter!

*

STAY WITH US - SAMPLE CHAPTER

As the last few shimmering rays of golden sunlight dipped below the horizon, Emilia's eyelids fluttered shut.

She tugged gently at the thick beach blanket draped loosely around her feet, pulling it up and over her bare legs, then she smiled and leaned to one side as she nuzzled her cheek into the nook of Amy's still warm shoulder.

The smoke from the little disposable barbecue drifted lazily over them both, catching in the eddy's of swirling wind and sand that whispered quietly in the dusk as the rhythmic pulse of the ocean waves crashed against the shore.

She was in heaven.

With her eyes still closed she took a deep breath, savouring the taste of the salty sea air on her tongue, and then she sank her feet into the soft white sand, wiggling her toes as she dug them deeper and deeper until her ankles felt damp and cool.

She loved moments like this.

There was nothing particularly remarkable about them, but

she knew them when they came. Fragments of life that would become a bubble of memory for years to come.

Ten years from now, she might be reading a good book in her favourite armchair - curled up with Amy she hoped - and her mind would drift, a memory jogged, and she'd be back here, now, in this very moment, feeling the kiss of the sun on one cheek and the warmth of her girlfriend's neck on the other.

Autumn was fast approaching as the searing heat of summer faded, each year feeling warmer and more uncomfortable than the last. Although Emilia loved spring and summer, with their warmth and colour and beauty, she *lived* for the winter and looked forward to Christmas with the unbridled joy and anticipation of a six year old girl.

Her parents had made every effort as she and her sister Alice had grown up, to make the holidays feel full of magic and joy, and that powerful childlike sensation of wonder had never faded. She wouldn't admit to it freely, but there was still a part of her that believed in Santa.

The fact of the matter was that she couldn't *disprove* his existence. How did she know he *didn't* really live at the North Pole in a beautiful log cabin, with a roaring fire surrounded by a stone fireplace frequented by tiny toy building elves?

She'd never been presented with compelling evidence to the contrary, and so with a wry smile and her tongue firmly in her cheek, the magic had stayed alive in some regressive corner of her mind and once every twelve months she let it loose.

For some reason - which Emilia suspected stemmed from her time in secondary school - Christmas always felt like it *began* after Halloween.

When the last day of the tenth month rolled around each year, her festive hat would be metaphorically pulled on and the lead up to Christmas Day would begin. So as the penultimate day of October faded from view, disappearing behind a long, flat and endless skyline, she felt that little jingle of excitement brewing in her chest.

Just over two months ago, she and her husband Cassian - and her now girlfriend Amy, and *her* husband Mark - had returned from France, having spent a hedonistic week fulfilling a bucket list of naughty fantasies together... and *apart*.

As it was, their holiday had marked the first time that she had made love *without* her husband, and that had turned out to be a quite remarkable milestone for more than one reason.

That first night - with Cassian back in England still - she had been taken tenderly and lovingly by Amy and Mark, and it had been more beautiful and fulfilling than she could ever have imagined.

At the same time, a thousand miles away on the other side of the Channel, her big sister Alice had turned up on her and her husband's doorstep looking for help and a place to stay.

Perhaps it had been something in the air that night... something *dangerous* and *exciting*. As though *Temptation herself* had laid down a challenge - a gauntlet that should have been, by all rights, *impossible* to navigate. Yet somehow they had managed it.

Her husband had slept with her sister.

Fucked her, to be precise, over their dining room table, and then again in their bed by all accounts.

And Emilia had given her *permission* for them to do it, and loved them all the more so *for* it.

She knew it should've felt wrong, but it *hadn't.* It was as though there was some disconnect in her brain that was preventing her from comprehending that.

But it *wasn't* a disconnect, it wasn't something *wrong* with her.

It was *her* way of loving them.

She had a big heart, and the more she loved, the more it seemed to grow. She loved Mark, she loved Amy. She also loved her husband, *and* she loved her sister.

If they wanted each other, who was she to say no? She didn't feel jealous when Amy and Mark made love, so why would it be different with Alice and Cassian? There was no question of forgiveness, there was nothing to forgive.

As they had boarded the plane on their last day in France, feeling both giddy and relaxed, she had felt intensely excited for them both.

From the moment Cassian had landed in France, flying out to join them and leaving Alice behind, she had sensed he had been longing to be back with her again, to explore their new relationship, their new found openness with one another, and she had been excited for him.

For *them*.

But by the time they'd returned, Alice had already left.

The last time they'd spoken she had been in Berlin.

They had both hoped that she would be home when they'd returned, and Emilia knew that Cassian had been disappointed. All the way back he'd been wide eyed and full of excitement and when they'd come through the front door to find her gone, he'd been crestfallen. He had hidden it well, and she'd understood, and if anything she'd felt sad *for* him.

Since then, they'd heard nothing.

Emilia had tried to call her on several occasions and Cassian had too, but each time it had gone straight to her voicemail... *Alice is in Wonderland right now, and can't get to the phone...*

A month had passed with no word.

It wasn't entirely unusual to not see her wayward and often chaotic sister for such a long time - she frequently travelled for work - but it was out of character to hear nothing at all, and the circumstances surrounding her sudden departure were making Emilia anxious. She knew it had been weighing on Cassian's mind too.

Where was she? Was she safe? Was she upset? Jealous? Angry? Had their encounter changed something within her? Perhaps ignited something inside of her that she wasn't ready to face?

And then there was Celeste...

She grinned as the memory of their passionate, desperate and delicate night together flashed back in her mind - *just her and her girls* - and she felt herself blush in the fading orange light.

Their vacation had been a week filled with lust, passion, taboo, and excitement. She had felt possessed, inflamed, intoxicated with love, fulfilled beyond her wildest dreams and completely besotted. But it had also been intense, confusing and bewildering at times. It had ended like their story had begun, with the four of them making love together, this time beneath the stars of a warm Mediterranean night.

And then, as they had awoken, naked and laying in each others arms in the makeshift four poster bed that Mark and Cassian had constructed in the grounds of their private villa, she had said something *crazy*.

Something that *now*, in the cold and fading autumnal light of England, seemed silly and rash.

She had told Amy and Mark - and her own husband - that she wanted them all to move in together... and to start a family.

The very thought of that moment made her tummy tingle in a way that made her feel both giddy and ashamed.

To her astonishment, they had said *yes*. Well, *Amy and Cassian* had said yes.

Mark, the voice of reason and rationality in their foursome, had said... *Maybe*.

And then nothing more had been said.

That had been the last word spoken on the matter.

Almost two months had passed, and not one of them had mentioned the idea again. It was as though they collectively knew that it had been a sentiment borne from passion and lust, gushed forth in the heat of the moment.

Something foolish.

They had known one another for just *three months*.

She didn't want to admit it, or accept it - to herself or to the others - but in that instant, and in all the anxiety ridden echoes of that moment... *something* had changed.

They all knew it.

Her words had changed everything, and it was now the elephant in the room.

It was like they had all been inflating a balloon, and with each puff it had grown and grown in size, becoming thinner and thinner, and less opaque, until finally it had reached maximum surface tension, and then Emilia had taken one final *deep* inhalation and *blown*... And they had all closed their eyes.

And waited.

Yet somehow, their little miracle balloon hadn't popped - it had stretched just that *little* bit further - but every one of them was still holding their breath.

Waiting.

It *had* to burst, it was only a matter of time, but no one wanted to be the one to do it.

So the idea had lingered, and their unconventional, and *wonderful* relationship had survived, and Emilia had breathed out... and relaxed.

Amy's hand slid down from her shoulder and came to a rest on her bottom, then it slipped inside the thin material edge of her bikini, making her grin and tingle. Beneath the blanket her fingers searched for her girlfriend's, finding them and clasping them, interlocking them affectionately and squeezing them tight.

'Do you want to stay with us tonight?' said Emilia softly, her heart pounding and her chest tightening as she spoke the words out loud.

Since they had returned from their holiday, the four of them had spent most evenings and nights together, but Emilia still found herself almost paralysed with anxiety and excitement whenever she would invite Amy and Mark to stay.

They rarely said no, and the invitations were always reciprocated and over time a natural balance and routine had nudged its way into their lives, but the initiation still felt taboo, and *deeply* arousing.

It still felt *new*.

And because it felt so right, she had to keep reminding herself that it *was* new. At just a few months old their relationship was barely in its infancy.

It was still naive and sweet, but at any moment, things could change.

Amy's hand squeezed hers beneath the blanket as she shifted her arm and pulled her closer. 'I was starting to think you were never going to ask.'

She smiled as she turned and looked across at her little redhead's face in the dwindling light.

Her emerald green eyes sparkled, reflecting the white crests of the waves as the maroon dusk light deepened and darkened, then she leaned in and kissed her delicately, letting her lips linger as they tasted each other.

Bliss.

As the sun set on the horizon, a cool wind blew in from the water, chilled by the waves and spreading out low and flat across the sand.

'I'm getting cold,' she said, shivering as she pulled away, dizzy with desire. 'Where are the boys?'

Amy looked up and across the beach, sweeping her gaze back and forth as she squinted in the half-light. In the distance, two men with familiar silhouettes were running side by side through the surf, cutting along the flat of the orange knife-edge horizon, and slowly making their way towards them.

'Over there I think,' said Amy, nodding as Emilia followed her gaze.

The four of them were among the last few hundred people remaining on the sand at this time of the evening. The glow of a dozen or more barbecues twinkled in her eyes as she looked out and focused on the two men.

'Are you sure that's them?'

'I think so?' said Amy. 'They look hot either way.'

Emilia laughed and shrugged. 'They'll do then, I guess?'

Amy nodded and squeezed her girlfriend tight.

Mark was an enigma, which Emilia had become certain, was an integral part of his irresistible charm. He was dark, undoubtedly formidable - he was a bodyguard after all - and he kept his emotions and feelings close to his chest. Stereotypically he should have been brimming with bravado and machismo, fiercely protective of his wife and swamped with jealousy at the unconventional relationship he had found himself in. Yet he had taken to it without any apparent hesitation, welcoming both of them into his life - and his bedroom - with understanding, compassion and love.

The more Emilia thought about it, the more she saw elements of herself within him. His love for Amy unconditional, much like hers for Cassian and Alice, and now him and Amy. Despite this, she still found him a mystery. At times it seemed like he was the only adult, and the three of them were the wayward adolescents, challenging decency, convention, and wisdom as he tried to corral them all - Amy, the hot wife, Emilia the crazy best friend, and Cassian the boy that looked up to him with puppy dog eyes. She laughed quietly to herself at the allegory.

It wasn't a fair assessment in truth, they each had their own strengths and their own weaknesses and together they were stronger, but Mark seemed to have assumed the position within their quad, of being the natural leader, and Emilia had to admit, that this was a deeply attractive quality.

Perhaps it was his military background, or simply his presence, but they looked to him for guidance, and waited for his say so, and in so many ways, she loved it.

She loved *him*, and all of them together, and the more and more complicated it had become, the more and more deathly afraid she was of it all falling apart.

'*Oi*,' said a whisper in her ear. 'Stop daydreaming, I can practically hear you dribbling.'

Suddenly Amy was pulling her backwards and down onto the beach towel behind them and running her fingers across her tummy, making her squeal and wriggle in delight.

'What are you doing?' she squeaked.

'I bet I can make you *come* before they get here.'

'What?' she said, her eyes wide with sudden panic. '*No*, don't you *da-*'

Emilia gasped, ushering a sharp intake of breath as Amy's slender fingers slid inside the still damp waistband of her bikini bottoms and grazed against her throbbing warmth, casting illicit trembles throughout her body as her eyes closed involuntarily.

'No?' said Amy arching one eyebrow and smiling as she froze, her finger curled back and waiting for permission like a tiger, ready to pounce.

Emilia bit her lip and looked around, craning her head back to see how far away the nearest people were as she breathed out and resisted the urge to thrust her hips up against Amy's poised hand.

Finally her eyes came back to the lithe little redhead and she nodded almost imperceptibly, her cheeks flushed with trepidation.

Try as she might, she could *never* resist this.

'Do your best to be quiet,' whispered Amy as she drew closer, her hot breath flushing against Emilia's cheek. Then her finger pressed down and she began to swirl steadily against her clit.

Want more? Treat yourself to a little alone time...

Buy Stay With Us now on Kindle or read it for free on Kindle Unlimited

*

THANK YOU

Thank you for reading **Come With Us!**

You can now **rate my books without leaving a review on Amazon**, but if you do have a few moments to spare, I'd love to hear your thoughts.

Even just a couple of lines makes a **HUGE** difference, and I would be so grateful. It really helps other amazing readers like yourself feel *confident* in giving a **new author a try.**

If you have the time to rate it, or leave a review on Goodreads or BookBub too, that would be incredible!

Follow me on Amazon, Twitter, Instagram, Goodreads & BookBub

Subscribe to my newsletter for all my latest news, new

releases and deals!

Read my brand new anthology series - First Time Swingers

In **Into the Swing**, Freya and Cameron meet Ash and Naomi, a gorgeous sexy couple who turn their lives upside down in one desperate, taboo and passion filled night that just might change everything… forever.

In **Back Swing**, Ashleigh and Claire and their husbands Noah and Jay, engage in an explosive game of truth or dare as they head to the sauna

In **Hot Swing**, Elina and Antonio invite Callie and Jack over for a night of fun and games in their brand new hot tub.

And in **Mistletoe Swing**, Ava and Max fly into New York City on Christmas Eve to visit best friends Bonnie and Logan, for one *very* special night, with *all* the trimmings.

'Sensual, dirty, and all sorts of sharing. You know what they say "Sharing is caring", and these couples share A LOT!'

Read my brand new anthology series on Kindle & Kindle Unlimited, and follow a whole host of new couples, expanding their horizons for the very first time as they begin to explore the swinger lifestyle.

Read the #1 Bestselling Taboo Fantasies Series

At first the idea was naughty and rude, but the more Elsie thought about it, the more it became lip bitingly tempting, shamefully arousing and skin-tinglingly taboo.

What starts as a taboo curiosity, quickly escalates into an overwhelming desire to push the conventional boundaries of their sex life, both in and out of the bedroom.

*'This was my **first**, and **definitely not last** read of Brianna Skylark… what are you trying to **DO** to me?! **THAT. WAS. HOT!!!***

*'This story is a **real breath of fresh air**. This is **super** sexy erotica. Careful where you read this one, folks!'*

*'Sensual, **stimulating**, seductive, beautiful and written with love. You can feel every push, every stretch!*

Read the ***number one bestselling series*** on Kindle & Kindle Unlimited, and follow loving and happily married couple

Brianna Skylark

Elsie and Cole as they explore, push and break the boundaries of their relationship with each new *super sexy, naughty story.*

Read the #1 Bestselling The Billionaire's Naked Cleaner Series

A mysterious billionaire, a shy hipster chick and a rebellious playboy hacker.

Sophie is broke, single and jobless. She's two weeks away from eviction and is facing the very real possibility of having to move back in with her country bumpkin parents. Then her best friend makes a throwaway comment that changes her life forever…

One day later and she's setup her own cleaning business, Sweet and Discreet. It's a one girl cleaning service with a naked twist.

Three clients, three very different encounters. All of them want her and with each sparkling visit, the tension escalates, surely it's only a matter of time before squeaky-clean Sophie gets down on her hands and knees… for some dirty fun.

'WOW! This builds from teasing to sensual, to downright ***scorching.'***

Read the ***number one bestselling series*** on Kindle & Kindle

Unlimited, and follow Sophie as her high-end client list quickly grows. With each new skin-tingling encounter becoming naughtier than the last, will she maintain her composure and remain professional… or will she succumb to temptation, curiosity and **raw naked attraction?**

*

ABOUT THE AUTHOR

BRIANNA SKYLARK is the pen name of a happily married, utterly insatiable, thirty-something mother of two living in a repressed little village on the south coast of England.

She's the wife of a rugged archeologist and often likes to think she's married to Indiana Jones. Over the years she's experimented with various occupations including filmmaking, video game voiceover artist and climbing instructor, but her favourite job is her most recent one... steamy romance novelist.

She loves bringing sweet, strong, faithful and loving women to life through her books, and then introducing them to strong, kind and endearing alpha males (or sensual females) who satisfy their every desire in the bedroom and beyond.

When she's not writing, she's often found hiking or climbing in the far reaches of Scotland and Wales or exploring the woods and beaches near her home with the man of her dreams, and their two gorgeous children.

Follow me on Amazon, Twitter, Instagram, Goodreads & BookBub

www.briannaskylark.com
Short, secret, sexy and sweet.

Printed in Great Britain
by Amazon

81800930R00130